The Campfire Crush

date him or dump him?

The Campfire Crush

A Choose Your Boyfriend Book

CYLIN BUSBY

BLOOMSBURY
CHILDREN'S
BOOKS

Published by Bloomsbury U.S.A. Children's Books
175 Fifth Avenue, New York, NY 10010
Distributed to the trade by Holtzbrinck Publishers

Library of Congress Cataloging-in-Publication Data
Busby, Cylin.
The campfire crush / by Cylin Busby. — 1st U.S. ed.
p.   cm.   — (Date him or dump him? A choose your boyfriend book ; 1)
Summary: As a junior counselor at a summer camp, the reader chooses whether to
try and rekindle a romance that was just getting started the previous year or start
dating someone new, while also dealing with a cabin full of young girls.
ISBN-13: 978-1-59990-083-4 • ISBN-10: 1-59990-083-1
1. Plot-your-own stories. [1. Camps—Fiction. 2. Dating (Social customs)—Fiction.
3. Plot-your-own stories.] I. Title.
PZ7.B9556Cam 2007   [Fic]—dc22   2006027974

First U.S. Edition 2007
Book designed and typeset by Amelia May Anderson
Printed in the U.S.A. by Quebecor World Fairfield
2 4 6 8 10 9 7 5 3 1

All papers used by Bloomsbury U.S.A. are natural, recyclable products
made from wood grown in well-managed forests. The manufacturing processes
conform to the environmental regulations of the country of origin.

BLOOMSBURY
CHILDREN'S
BOOKS

For Melanie and Stacy
Choose well, ladies.

The
Campfire
Crush

As your parents pull out of the parking lot, you're a little sad…for about two seconds. Every year, it's the same thing. Lots of minivans, sad-looking moms saying goodbye to their kids, and the campers with their huge backpacks and sleeping bags all lining up to get on the buses. It's almost like time stands still from one year to the next. Except this year, one thing is different—*really* different. You're not just another camper; you're a counselor. (Well, a junior counselor, but still!)

Then you see Missy, your best camp friend, pulling her gear out of her parents' car, and she spots you, too. "Hey!" she screams, jumping up and down. It's been about nine months since you've seen each other.

"You look different," you have to admit, taking in the suddenly tall and super pretty girl in front of you. "When did you get your braces off?"

"Three weeks ago." Missy grins big, showing you her perfect white teeth. "It's the best—I'm so happy. You look different, too," Missy says, looking you up and down. "In a good way, a *really* good way! I can't wait to see what Seth does when he lays eyes on you!" She giggles.

You feel yourself blushing. "Who knows if he's even going to be here this year…I mean, did you hear that he was?"

Just then, a piercing whistle cuts through the crowd.

2

"Oh no," you whisper to Missy, eyeing a tall, severe-looking woman with a clipboard standing by the bus. She has her trademark silver whistle on a cord around her neck, just like last year and the year before that.

"It's the Skunk!" Missy whispers back. Your least favorite camp leader is back for another year—Ms. Sally, aka the Skunk Lady—not that she smells, but her jet-black hair has a big streak of white in the front. And, as with a skunk, you have to be really careful around her, because she can turn on you in a minute.

"Hello, girls," Ms. Sally says stiffly to you and Missy. She looks down at her clipboard. "Junior counselors this year?"

"Yup," Missy says, unable to hide her enthusiasm. "We're really excited to meet our campers and—"

"How nice for you." Ms. Sally cuts her off. "Now why don't you get excited about loading this gear on the bus; that's the duty of the junior counselors." Ms. Sally points to a huge pile of backpacks and sleeping bags.

As you start loading the heavy bags, Missy groans, "I thought being a counselor would be fun, but so far..." She looks at the pile of bags and lets out a sigh.

"You guys need a hand?" a voice says from behind you. You turn and lock onto the bluest eyes you've ever seen.

"Uh, yeah," you say, almost stuttering. He's tall, blond—and totally out of your league.

"Absolutely," Missy agrees.

"I'm Rob," he says. "I'm a counselor for the boys' camp this year." You watch as he lifts two heavy bags and tosses them into the bus with ease. He's got to be older; the guys at your school do not have arms like that.

3

"What school do you guys go to?" Rob asks, lifting another bag.

"I'm at Marlborough, the girls' school," Missy says, and you tell him the name of your school, too.

Rob stops and stands up for a second, wiping his hands on the front of his jeans. "High school?" he says, looking skeptical, and his eyes meet yours for a split second, making you feel a little dizzy. "Oh..." He bends and picks up a few bags. "I thought...well, I'm starting college in the fall."

You and Missy exchange a quick glance, and she mouths the word "hot." You stifle a giggle and keep loading the bags. With Rob's help, you're finished in minutes.

4   "I'll see you guys there, I guess," Rob says awkwardly as he heads for his bus.

"Absolutely," Missy says. "And Rob? Thanks for the help." She gives him a big, perfect smile.

"You and that new smile of yours!" you joke with her as you climb onto the girls' bus; then you see the mayhem in front of you and stop laughing. The bus is full of girls—all kinds of girls, from age seven and up, and they all seem to be talking at once. Pigtails flying here, a princess outfit there; one girl is trying to put on nail polish while the younger ones are actually jumping on seats. It's a madhouse.

"Uh...," Missy says, taking in the scene.

Ms. Sally's whistle cuts though the noise as she comes up the stairs behind you. "Girls," she says, looking at you and Missy. "You need to help me get the campers in line!"

You and Missy just stand there, not knowing what to do, so Ms. Sally takes over. "THAT'S ENOUGH!" she hollers in her booming voice, and the bus falls silent. "Get into your seats now! I'm counting to three!" Every girl on the bus scrambles. Missy grabs a seat near the front and you slide in next to her as Ms. Sally begins to rattle off the rules for the ride. "There will be NO standing while the bus is in motion..."

It's the same speech she's given every year, but this year it's a little different. Because this year, you're not hearing it as an unruly camper, but as a counselor—someone who's supposed to be in charge. "Were we this crazy when we were campers?" Missy whispers to you. You can only shake your head and look out the window as the bus rolls slowly from the

5

parking lot. "All I have to say is thank goodness we'll at least be together, right?" Missy asks.

"A cabin full of crazy girls, by myself? No, thanks!" you agree.

"And thank goodness that the boys' camp is so close," Missy says slyly.

"And that our new friend Rob is so very helpful," you add.

"Rob?" Missy raises her eyebrows. "Once we get to camp and you see Seth, you'll forget all about Mr. Biceps."

You look out the window and watch as the town falls away behind you, giving way to trees and the countryside, lush and green. You hate to admit it, but Missy is right. There's just something about Seth, or at least, there was something last summer—a spark between you. Unless you just imagined it all.

"Do you think Seth's going to be a junior counselor this year, too?" you ask Missy.

"I might know something," she says, a little grin on her face. "But don't you think it's so much better to be surprised?"

You have to smile—it's great to be back hanging out with Missy. This is going to be an amazing summer. The two of you catch up on everything that happened over the school year during the hour-long trip, and before you know it, the bus is turning down the dirt road lined with tall pine trees that will end at the lake, and Camp Butterfield. The small log cabins surround one side of the lake, the boys' camp over on the right, the girls' camp on the left. The main hall, where all the meals are served—and all the parties and dances are held!—sits right in the middle, between the boys' and girls' camps.

"All right, campers," Ms. Sally says as the doors swing open. "Off the bus in a single file and line up according to cabin; then you can get your bags and settle in."

Some of the campers look so young, you can't believe their parents would let them come here alone. You and Missy do your best to get the girls lined up and into groups.

"Let's get you into a line," you say to one girl, who looks about nine years old.

"You're not my counselor; you can't boss me around," she snaps back, chewing her gum loudly. Her name tag says her name is Sofie.

You're about to say something to her when Ms.

Sally toots her whistle and says, "I need all the girls' camp counselors over here. Now."

You and Missy exchange a look and gather with the other counselors near the bus. "Unfortunately, one of our counselors has broken her leg and won't be joining us. That means we are one counselor short. I need a volunteer to be the sole counselor of the seven- and eight-year-olds cabin," Ms. Sally says, pointing to the cabin on the edge of the lake, nearest the boys' camp. "Anyone?"

You look over to the cabin, and you see him—it's Seth! He's taller, even cuter than last year, but it's him for sure! And he's moving his campers into the cabin right next to the one Ms. Sally is offering up for grabs.

You look around the group of counselors. A few of them look older than you and Missy, but everyone here is probably hoping to be in a cabin with a friend—not going it alone. "Erin, you up for it?" Ms. Sally asks a pale pretty girl with long black hair. She looks old enough to be in college. "No, thanks, Ms. Sally," Erin answers. "I want to stay with Natalie this summer." She gives the girl standing next to her a big smile.

"How nice for you," Ms. Sally says sarcastically. "Anyone else? How about you?" Ms. Sally asks, pointing at you. You bite your lip for a second to think. You could either share a cabin—and the counselor responsibilities—with Missy, or take a chance on running a cabin of campers all by yourself—right next door to the boys' camp.

"Well? I'm waiting," Ms. Sally says impatiently. You look over at Missy—if you took the job being a solo counselor, you'd still see her at activities. And you'd be right next door to Seth. But it just wouldn't be the same as being in one cabin and doing the job together—that's the whole reason you decided to take the counselor job in the first place. So you...

9

Decide to take the job and be a counselor alone. Go to 125.

Think you'd rather share the counselor job with Missy.

Go to 10.

"Fine," Ms. Sally says. "I'll have to be the counselor for that cabin myself, I guess." Her eyes shift to you with a cold glare. It seems like she was counting on you! Great, now you'll have to watch your back for the rest of the summer!

You and Missy will be the counselors for the nine-year-olds cabin, so you get your girls in line and head over to the cabin. Missy leads the group of six girls, and you walk behind, remembering back to when you were nine—your first year at camp!

You're lost in a daydream when someone steps in front of you—it's Seth!

"Hey, you're a junior counselor this year?" he asks.

"Yeah, the nine-year-olds," you tell him, meeting his hazel eyes. His dark hair is shorter but otherwise he's the same adorable guy from last summer. You feel your heart start to beat fast.

"Um," he says awkwardly, looking down. "That's cool, great, I mean, it's really good that you're going to be here this summer."

You're glad that he's feeling as uncomfortable as you are! Just then, Missy interrupts.

"Hey, let's go!" She's standing with your group of campers, who are waiting for you to finish up your conversation.

"One minute," you tell her, and she puts a hand on her hip, looking exasperated.

You turn back to Seth. "I'm glad you're here this summer, too," you say; then you both stand there just looking at each other for a second. "Well, I guess I better get my campers in their cabin," you finally say as you move away from him.

"Wait, do you maybe want to hang out or something? You know, catch up?" he suddenly asks.

"Yeah." You smile. "When?"

"How about now?" He grins. "Meet you at the lake in five minutes, okay?"

Missy lets out a loud sigh and taps her foot. All the campers are getting tired of waiting, too—one girl has even put her bag on the ground and is sitting on it. "Come on!" Missy says, widening her eyes at you. You decide to ...

Join Seth at the lake and let Missy get the girls settled in to the cabin. Go to 12.

Go with Missy and the girls and do your job. Go to 14.

"*L*et's meet in five minutes!" You tell Seth.

Once you get the campers and all their gear into the cabin, you turn to Missy and whisper, "He wants me to meet him at the lake!"

"Great," Missy says sarcastically. "Look, I'm really happy for you that Seth is here, but we're supposed to get our campers settled in now, not hang out with guys."

"Counselor, can you help me?" asks one very shy little redheaded girl in your cabin who clearly cannot figure out how to make her bed.

"Those aren't your sheets," Sofie says, grabbing them from her. "They're mine. That's my bunk, next to my best friend." You notice she has long red nails, which seem a little odd on a nine-year-old.

The redheaded girl looks ready to burst into tears; obviously she didn't come here with any friends—and you remember what that feels like all too well.

"Okay, let's find you some other sheets, and another bunk," you tell her, looking at her name tag. "Alice?"

She nods her head silently, tears welling up in her eyes. You find the only empty bunk, a top one in the corner, and climb up to help her make her bed, but one glance at your watch tells you that it's time to meet Seth, if you're going to do it.

"Here you go," you say to Alice. "I think you can take it from here." You climb down from the bunk. Missy gives you a look as you open your bag and take out your swimsuit. "I'll be back," you say over your shoulder as you head out the door.

"Wait a second," Missy says, catching your arm. "You've got to be kidding me! I need your help here." She points to Alice, who is now sitting on her unmade bed, crying quietly.

"But Seth—," you say, looking down toward the lake, where he's waiting for you. He's standing on the dock in his swim trunks, with a towel slung over one shoulder. You...

13

Stay with Missy and help with the girls. Go to 16.
Join Seth at the lake for a swim. Go to 19.

You're a little bummed that you had to blow Seth off, but it's just not the right time.

When you reach the cabin, you notice the door is open a bit—that's strange, since Ms. Sally had given you a key and it's supposed to be locked. You push open the door.

"Anyone here?" you ask, but the cabin is empty.

"Okay, you guys," you tell your campers, "come on in."

The first girl to push past you is the tiny blond with long red nails named Sofie. "I'm getting the best bunk," she announces to everyone. "And this one," she says, pointing to the bunk next to it, "is for my best friend, Sky." She turns to a quiet girl behind her with long dark braids.

"Don't touch any of my stuff," Sofie says to the group as she starts to unpack. You notice that her suitcase is designer, expensive, and packed with all kinds of things that she'll never use at camp—makeup, nail polish, fancy dress shoes.

You and Missy exchange a look and a smirk.

"AHHHHHHHHHHHHHHHHHH!" Sofie yells suddenly. "It's a snake! It's a snake! It's on my bed!"

Under her pile of sheets, a big black snake is sitting, coiled up. He looks asleep, until all the girls start screaming together—then he raises his head and looks around the cabin with his beady black eyes—and flicks his tongue out at you with a hiss!

"Oh no," you say, backing away from the bunk. All the campers have run to the other side of the cabin.

"DO something!" Sofie orders you. "It's on my BED!" she yells.

"Calm down, everyone!" Missy tells the girls, then turns to you and whispers, "What do we do?"

15

Try to catch the snake yourself. Go to 40.
Go and ask for help. Go to 55.

"Okay, you're right," you admit to Missy, and put your swimsuit back. You climb up to Alice's bunk and help her finish up her bed, then show her where to unpack her things. When you're done, she grabs your hand and quietly whispers, "Thanks, Counselor." You just smile back, knowing that you did the right thing staying in the cabin to help the campers, even though it was hard to blow off Seth and you hope he'll understand. Maybe you'll get to see him later.

The girls are almost done unpacking when the dinner bell rings out. "Time to eat!" Missy announces. "Let's line up, ladies."

As you follow the girls over to the dining hall, you notice that another camper is walking beside Alice—maybe she'll make a friend her first day here? You hope so, but if not, she can sit with you and Missy at dinner.

The bulletin board outside the dining hall is already filling up with notices about the different activities at camp, and you notice Rob—the hot guy who helped you and Missy load the bus—is putting up one.

"Hey," you say with a little wave.

"Hey, yourself," he says back, locking eyes with you again. "You into whitewater rafting?" He points to the sign he's posting.

"I don't know," you admit as another guy walks up next to you.

"Excuse me," he says to you, "can I just hang this up here?" You move out of his way so that he can put up another sign—this one about a horseback riding trip.

"Horseback riding, huh?" you say, looking at the sign. "And a picnic. Sounds nice."

"Yeah," the guy says back, nodding awkwardly. He's wearing glasses that are a little too big for his face and he's kinda short—or maybe he just looks short next to Rob. You notice his name tag reads "Eli."

"You ride?" he asks you.

"A little." You shrug.

"But she's whitewater rafting with me tomorrow, right?" Rob says, looking at you.

"Well, I'll have to ask my campers what they want to do," you say.

17

"You and your co-counselor can split up—let her take half the campers on one trip, and you can take the other half on another trip," Eli suggests.

"That's a good idea." You nod.

"I'm going in," Rob says—and he seems annoyed. "Am I going to see you tomorrow or what?" Every time his eyes meet yours, you feel like you have to look away—fast—or you won't be able to speak.

"Um," you say, trying to think. Rob is cute, but he's got to be five years older than you—your parents would not be happy about you hanging out with a guy who's about to start college. And the horseback trip sounds really fun, almost better than whitewater rafting. You decide to...

18

Go on the whitewater-rafting trip to be with Rob. Go to 32.
Go on the horseback ride and picnic. Go to 141.

You put on your swimsuit. "Sorry," you say over your shoulder to Missy as you head out the door. "I promise I'll be back soon and help you take the campers over to dinner."

"Don't bother!" Missy yells, slamming the door behind you. You feel bad, but there's just no way you're going to miss this opportunity to hang with Seth!

When he hears your feet on the dock, he turns around and gives you a big grin. "I thought maybe you weren't coming," he says.

"I just had to help out the campers a little bit," you explain. "I mean, it is my job, right?" Suddenly, you're feeling really guilty for leaving Missy alone with the girls on the first day. But then Seth reaches for your hand. "I didn't realize until I saw you today how much I missed you. Why didn't we stay in touch?"

You just shake your head. "I don't know, busy, I guess?" You want to tell him that you thought a lot about him over the school year, but the words get stuck in your throat and instead you end up standing there staring at each other.

"It's hot; let's jump in!" he says finally.

"Do you think it's okay?" you ask, still feeling a little guilty. "I mean, we *are* supposed to be in our cabins right now."

"What happened to that fun girl I knew last summer?" Seth teases you, his hazel eyes sparkling. "I don't remember you being so worried about rules."

"Okay," you say reluctantly just as he jumps off the dock, making a big, loud splash in the water below.

You drop your towel and jump in after him, coming up just a few inches from where he's standing in waist-deep water.

"I like that suit," he says, looking at your bikini. "Looks good on you." Then he climbs back up onto the dock. "Let's jump together!" he says, pulling you up as well.

You're game, so you stand beside him and you both count to three, then jump in, holding hands. But when you come up, you feel something slippery slide by your foot—a fish? No, it's your bikini top!

"Oh no! My top!" you yell.

Seth starts laughing. "Let me see if I can find it," he says, putting his head under the water.

"NO!" you yell, worried that he might see something else under there.

He comes up smiling big. "Nothing yet," he says, taking a deep breath as he goes under again.

"Seth, DON'T!" you yell, a little too loud. Then you hear that whistle—it's the Skunk! She's standing on the dock watching you both.

"What on Earth are you doing in the water? Out. Now!" she orders.

Seth climbs onto the dock fast. "Sorry, Ms. Sally," he starts to say.

"I cannot believe this—we haven't even been here an hour, and two of my junior counselors are already breaking the rules? This is ridiculous! Get out now," she says, pointing to you. "*Right* now."

"I can't," you start to explain. "I've lost my top in the water."

"Oh, you *lost* it, did you?" Ms. Sally says, looking skeptical. "Indeed. I don't like liars, little miss, and I don't trust you with MY campers. Your summer here is *over*. Pack your things and call your parents to come and get you." With that, she turns on her

Birkenstock and marches back to the office as you burst into tears.

"Sorry," Seth says, and walks off the dock, leaving you in the water alone.

You finally muster up the courage to climb onto the dock and wrap up—fast!—in your towel before anyone sees. Walking back to the cabin, you wonder how you're going to explain to your parents that you were fired—and why. Ugh.

END

Want to go back and try this whole day over again? Go to 10.

You decide to race over to Seth's cabin to ask him for help—why not? He can help you guys with the snake, and it's a good excuse to see him again!

"Seth!" you yell the second you see him. "I need your help—it's an emergency!"

"What's up?" he says.

"There's a snake in our cabin!" you say breath-lessly.

You hear a few laughs from his campers, and from his co-counselor. "A snake?" Seth says. "What do you want me to do?" he asks, looking a little annoyed.

"Well, can you help us get it out of the cabin, or something?" you fumble.

"I guess," he says with a shrug. "I'll be right back," he says to his campers.

"You get 'im, snake killer," his co-counselor jokes.

Maybe this wasn't such a great idea. You two walk quickly back to your cabin in silence, and when you get there, all the girls are standing outside, squealing.

"There's a giant snake in there!" Sofie says, terrified.

"Yeah, I heard," Seth says sarcastically as he opens the door. After a few minutes he comes out holding a paper bag.

"Got 'im," he says, and all the girls squeal and scatter. "What is it with you girls and snakes? It's really not that big a deal." Seth looks totally exasperated. "I've got to get back to my campers." He turns to you and says, "Are you going to the campfire tonight?"

You were psyched to go and to see him there, but now you're not so sure. It seems like Seth has changed a lot over the past year—he used to be a really sweet guy, but now he's acting so distant.

You decide to...

Give him another chance and agree to meet him at the campfire. Go to 27.

Skip the campfire so that you don't have to see him. Go to 29.

You race out the door and head over to the office, where you find Ms. Sally.

"We have a snake!" you exclaim. "It's on a bed in the cabin."

For the first time ever, you see Ms. Sally look a little frightened. "A snake?" she says, her voice shaking, "Oh, I hate snakes! Let me grab Joey. He'll help us."

She heads out the door and you follow her over to a cabin in the boys' camp. "Joey, I need your help. A snake—," Ms. Sally says, talking to a tall, skinny guy inside.

"I'm on it," Joey says quickly, coming down the stairs. "Hi," he says, stopping to look at you for a second before turning to follow Ms. Sally. He's cute, in a nerdy way—sorta not your type, with crazy curly hair and hippy sandals. But he seems nice.

When you get to the cabin, all the girls are standing outside squealing, including Missy. Ms. Sally surprises you by joining the group and looking really terrified. "I just hate snakes," she says again.

Joey heads inside, and in a few minutes comes out holding the snake in his bare hands! The girls all scream and run off in every direction. "Don't worry, I'm taking him over to the woods," Joey explains as he heads for the thick bushes and trees that line the camp.

"Okay, girls, into the cabin," Ms. Sally orders, back to her old self again.

As the girls file inside, Joey heads over to your cabin. "Hi, I'm Joey," he says to Missy.

"Hi," Missy says, and introduces herself. You notice her blushing a little. Maybe she thinks Joey is kinda cute, too. He's definitely a super brave guy.

"So, are you two going to the campfire tonight?" he asks, looking right at you. This guy is not your type, but there is just something about him that's really adorable. You look over and see Missy gazing at him, too.

"I'm going," she says fast. "Want to sit together?"

You're a little surprised and decide to ...

26

Also go to the campfire—who says she has dibs on Joey? You saw him first! Go to 38.

Skip the campfire and give Missy a solo chance with this cutie. Go to 29.

$\mathcal{B}$efore heading to the campfire with your campers that evening, you decide to change into a cute new pair of shorts and put on a little lip gloss—just in case. Seth was kind of a jerk to you earlier in the day, but you're going to give him another chance.

When you get there, you see Seth sitting with another guy, who you recognize as his co-counselor. "Hey!" Seth waves you over to sit by him. "This is Eric," he says, pointing to his friend.

"Hey," Eric says, nodding at you. "Got that problem in your cabin all squared away?" You have to laugh, realizing that maybe it wasn't the emergency you thought it was.

The campers all sit in groups around the fire and toast marshmallows while an older counselor starts telling ghost stories. In one story, a little girl goes swimming in the lake after dark, even though her parents told her not to. She drowns in the lake and then her ghost comes back to haunt anyone who swims at night. You feel yourself moving a little closer to Seth as the story gets really scary.

"You're not scared, are you?" Seth asks suddenly. You think about it for a second...

You are scared. Go to 60.

Ghost stories don't spook you. Go to 138.

To get out of going to the campfire that night, you pretend to have a stomachache, sending the campers off to the campfire without you.

A few minutes after they all leave, you hear a knock on the door—it's Ms. Sally. "I heard that you're ill," she says, feeling your forehead. "If you have a stomach virus, I don't want it sweeping through the whole camp. You need to go to the infirmary and see the nurse."

You open your mouth to tell her that you were just pretending, but then think better of it and agree to follow her to the infirmary. When you get there, the nurse takes your temperature and your pulse. "You seem to be okay," she says. "I don't think it's the flu. Why don't you lie down for a while and let's see if you feel better?" she says, leading you into another room where there are several cots set up. There's a blond guy sitting on one cot reading a magazine.

"What are you in for?" he asks, shooting you a grin.

"Stomachache," you tell him, sitting down on the cot next to his. "You?"

"Poison oak," he explains, pulling up his sleeve to show you an angry red rash on his arm. "It's all over me, and it's pretty bad. What's your name?" he asks, so you tell him and then find out that his name is Gus Butterfield.

"Oh, just like the camp," you say, then realize what it means.

"Yeah, my parents kinda own it." He shrugs, looking a little embarrassed.

"Your parents *own* the camp?" you ask him.

"This one and a couple of others…oh, and a hotel, and an amusement park, too." He looks away, and it's clear he doesn't really want to talk about it anymore, so you change the subject.

"What are you reading?" you ask him, and he shows you his magazine—it's about karate and martial arts. "I'm into tae kwon do," he says. "Wanna see some moves?" Before you know it, he's jumped up to show you some martial arts moves— and he's actually pretty good! It's when he starts adding the comic book sound effects that you have to laugh. "POW, *ker-chow*," he says, swinging his leg high and shooting out one fist as if fighting

30

off several opponents. "And check out this one," he says, letting out a long "Hi-YA!" as he jumps up quickly and lands in a new split-leg position.

Just then the nurse comes back in. "I thought I heard laughing in here," she says, looking at you. "You must be feeling much better. You ready to go back to your cabin now?"

You pretend that you're still sick so that you can hang out with Gus more. Go to 47.

You tell her that you feel better and leave. Go to 49.

The next morning, you and your campers walk down to the river to meet everyone else for the whitewater-rafting trip. The first person you see is Rob, standing on the river's edge with an oar in his hand, giving a demonstration to some other campers. Even in a puffy orange life jacket, you have to admit the guy is hot—there's just something about him. His light blue eyes meet yours for a second as you step down onto the rocks and he gives you a look.

"I'm glad you could make it," he says, stepping over to you. "Really glad. You and your campers will go in the same boat with me, okay?"

"Sure," you say back. When you're standing this close to him, you can't help but be reminded that he's a lot older than you—he's so tall and he has stubble on his cheeks.

"Okay, everyone in a life vest, please! It's going to be mostly Class Two rapids, but maybe a Class Three," Rob yells out over the group. "And remember, please sit in the back of the boat if you are a beginner. The front of the boat is dangerous and only for folks who have experience with whitewater rafting. Do not try to show off—you will get thrown from the boat and might even get hurt. Got it?" he asks the campers around him, and everyone nods.

You help your campers scramble into the big inflated raft, checking everyone to make sure they have their life vests on the right way. After all, you're in charge of them and want them to be safe. When it's your turn to climb aboard, Rob takes your hand. "Here, let me help you," he says. "I need one counselor up front, and one in the back." You glance at your campers sitting in a row in the back of the boat, where Rob said it would be safe. Do you dare to sit up front, just to be next to him?

33

You sit in the front of the boat to be near Rob, even though it's dangerous. Go to 41.

You sit in the back of the boat to help keep your campers safe. Go to 42.

"I'm ready," you tell Rob, and look him right in the eyes to show him that you're not scared.

"Okay." Rob sighs. Suddenly, he seems like he's annoyed with you. Isn't this what he wanted? You don't have any time to think about it as he pushes the boat off from the rocks and you guys head into the middle of the river, where the current picks up.

You watch how Rob uses the oar and try to copy him, but it's harder than it looks, and your hands start hurting almost right away. The boat ends up turning a little bit to the side with each stroke you take.

"Come on, you have to pull harder," Rob says to you. "Keep the boat straight!" He's practically yelling at you. You can't really keep up with him—your big puffy life vest keeps getting in the way of your arms. When you finally get your oar in the water the right way, the current pulls the boat along, making things a little easier, but by then your hands are raw and sore, and the hot sun is beating down on you.

"I have to take this off," you say, pulling the straps of your life vest. "It's too hot."

"NO!" Rob yells. "Do *not* take off your vest. You obviously know nothing about rafting." He shakes his head and stares out at the river, which is now moving fast around the boat.

He turns to you and says suddenly, "Here's our first drop. Can you at least *try* to help me keep the raft straight?"

Before you know what's happening, the water drops out from under the boat, then comes back up to meet it with a loud *whoosh!* and a huge splash. You're soaked through as water rushes over the boat.

"AAHHHHHHHHH!" Your campers are yelling from the back of the boat; they're having a blast just holding on for the ride.

"Here's another one," you hear Rob say, but it's too late, and suddenly you feel the oar being pulled from your hands by the current. You reach over the side to grab it, knowing that Rob will be so angry with you for dropping it, and—*whoosh!* You're hit with another big splash…and you're in the water! You've gone over the side, and the current is taking you downstream with it!

"Help!" you yell, but Rob and your campers in the boat have pulled ahead—they can't even reach you. You put out your hand to try and grab a rock, but you're moving so fast, you end up bashing your fingers instead. Ouch! Just then, you feel yourself lifted from the water—a counselor in the other boat is behind you, lifting you up into their raft.

"You okay?" he asks you, looking into your face.

"I guess so, but my hand," you say, holding it out—your fingers really hurt.

"You must have hit a rock in the water," he says. "You really took a tumble!"

Rob has maneuvered the other boat over to the shore at the side of the river and is waiting. When the boat you're in pulls up alongside, you can see that he's not happy.

"She's hurt. We have to take her back to camp," the other counselor tells Rob.

"Great, there goes the whole trip," Rob grumbles.

"I'm really sorry—," you start to explain.

"Save it," Rob cuts you off. "You're going home anyway. Ms. Sally won't allow an injured counselor, and it looks like your hand is pretty bad."

You look down at your swollen fingers and have to agree. Your crush on Rob and any hope of a perfect summer have just been washed down the stream.

END

Want to try sitting at the back of the boat? Go back to 32.

That night, as you and Missy are getting ready for the campfire, she slips on a pair of cool, faded jeans that show off her curves. "Do you think Joey will like these?" she asks you.

"I don't know," you say back, looking in your suitcase for something cute to wear. "I guess we'll have to find out what his type is."

"What do you mean?" Missy asks. "You think I'm not his type?"

"I'm just saying we don't know which one of us he's into," you say, not wanting to start a fight.

"Well, he asked *me* to the campfire, so I guess he's into me," Missy says, putting her hands on her hips.

"He asked *us* to the campfire," you point out.

"You've got to be kidding me," Missy exclaims. "You're not *seriously* going to make a move for the guy I like, are you?"

"I think we just need to see what happens," you tell her.

"No, we don't need to see," she says angrily. "I'm

telling you right now, I like him. If you make a move for him, we're not friends anymore. That's final." She meets your eyes, and you can tell she's absolutely serious. So you...

Decide your friendship with her is too important to mess up over a guy. Go to 50.

Still want to see what might happen with Joey. Go to 52.

You walk over to the bed slowly, very slowly, looking around for something to put the snake in. Maybe an empty trash can—you could trap it underneath, then go get help? Or a bag? As you move slightly closer, the snake stirs again.

"Don't get too close!" Missy says, terrified. "We don't know what kind of snake it is—it could be poisonous." All the campers are standing behind her, huddled together.

"I just want to get it trapped," you say, easing in closer—when suddenly it moves.

"AAAAAAAAHHHHHHHHHHHHHHHHH!" Sofie is screaming again, and then all the campers are screaming together.

"Let's get out of here!" Missy yells, and you all tumble outside as fast as you can.

"It didn't bite you, did it?" Missy looks at your arm for marks.

"Almost!" you admit, your hands still shaking.

Go to 55.

"Are you sure you want to sit *here*?" Rob says, looking at you seriously. "It can be dangerous—do you have any experience?"

"Sure," you say nonchalantly, sliding next to him.

"Okay," he says, shaking his head a little. He hands you an oar. "Then you must know how to use this, right?" he asks you.

You take the oar and hold it the same way he's holding his. "Got it," you say, trying to sound confident. After all, how hard could it be? Maybe he likes girls who are willing to take chances—you're betting he does.

"Here," he points out, "you need to hold it like this." He adjusts the oar in your hands, turning it over. "You're really sure you've got this? You can sit in the back and I'll have Erin come up here," he says, pointing to the pretty, older counselor who took the back seat with the campers.

You pause for a second, then decide…

41

You'd rather sit in the back of the boat. Go to 42.

You're staying where you are. Go to 34.

You climb into the back of the boat, feeling a little silly—you really wanted to be next to Rob, but it sounds a bit too risky for you.

"Ready?" you say to your campers as Rob pushes off from the shore.

"I'm scared," Sofie whines, looking at you. She's wearing a designer swimsuit under her life vest and her hair is blown out and curled. "I don't want to get my hair wet!"

You have to laugh. "Sofie, I think that you should have gone horseback riding this morning," you tell her.

Soon Rob has eased the boat to the mouth of the river, where the current picks up and carries you fast. But Rob knows exactly what to do, and even though you're a little bit scared when the boat almost tips over once, you end up having the best time ever. It's fun getting to know the campers— and watching Rob's back as he rows and steers the boat isn't bad either!

"I hate whitewater rafting!" Sofie yells as a wave

crashes over the raft, soaking you all. But everyone else has a blast getting totally drenched.

When you get back to the dock, Rob helps all the campers out of the boat, then takes your hand. "You did great," he says, his light blue eyes on yours for a second.

"Me? You're the one who did great. That was amazing, thanks!" You take off your life vest and toss it in the boat.

"So," Rob says. "Are you going to the dance on Friday? I mean, do you want to go? With me?"

It sounds like he's asking you on a date! He's hot, but you know he's way too old for you, and your parents wouldn't like you dating a college guy. So you tell him...

43

"I like you, but you're too old for me." Go to 61.
"I'd love to!" Go to 137.

"I'm a little bit scared," you admit to Seth.

"I knew you were. You're such a baby," Seth scoffs. "Right?" he says, turning to his friend.

"Actually, I'm a little scared, too," Eric admits, looking you in the eye for a second. You hadn't noticed him before—he's been pretty quiet all night. But now you realize that he's actually kinda cute and has really warm brown eyes.

Seth takes a stick and starts poking the campfire. "Great, I'm stuck sitting with *two* babies. I'm going to get some more marshmallows," he grumbles, and walks off.

Eric moves over to sit next to you, where Seth had been. "Your first year as a counselor?" he asks you.

You nod, then ask, "You?"

"Yup," he says. "Looks like it's going to be a lot of hard work. Are you doing the lifeguard training thing tomorrow?"

"I don't know," you tell him. "Are you?"

"I was thinking about it. But if you're going to do

it, I definitely want to be there," he says, looking into your face. Maybe it's just the light from the fire, but he's suddenly looking really cute to you. But you're still feeling a little hung up on Seth—after all, you did have a huge crush on him all last year. Do you give Seth another chance, or take Eric up on his offer?

You say…

"Okay, let's meet at lifeguard training." Go to 63.

"Sorry, I'm hanging out with Seth tomorrow." Go to 65.

"I'm not scared," you tell Seth. "They're just stupid stories, right?"

"Exactly," Seth agrees.

"I'm a little scared," Eric admits, looking at you. You notice for the first time that he's kinda cute, with really nice brown eyes.

"You're such a wuss!" Seth says to Eric. "A girl isn't even afraid of these dumb ghost stories and you are? He's a baby, right?" Seth turns to you and asks.

You agree with Seth and tease Eric. Go to 67.

You decide Seth is being mean and take Eric's side. Go to 68.

"I'll be back in a couple of hours to check on you two," the nurse says on her way out. Gus jumps up off his cot. "We've got this place to ourselves. Awesome!" He goes over to an old radio on the counter and turns it on to a rock station. "Come on," he says to you. "Let me teach you some tae kwon do moves!"

He strikes a pose, then says, "You try it."

When you do, you can't get your foot just right. "Here..." He positions your body. "That's it, now turn your head this way." He touches your cheek for a second and sends a shiver down your spine. "You've got it!"

After teaching you a couple more moves, you both climb into your cots and just talk in the dark. By the time the nurse comes back, you're almost asleep.

In the morning, you wake up scratching your face. Why is your cheek so itchy? You run to the bathroom and see a horrible rash across your face, your neck, and your arms... Gus has given you his poison oak!

You come back into the room and wake him up, "Look at this!" you practically yell at him. "I've got it now, too!"

"Oh no," Gus says. "Listen, promise me that you won't tell my girlfriend you got it from me, okay?"

You've got poison oak—he's got a girlfriend; a lousy start to the summer is written all over your face! If only you could do it all again, maybe you wouldn't have lied about that stomachache...

END

48

Want to do it all over again? Go back to 29.

"Well, I hope you feel better soon," you tell Gus on your way out of the infirmary.

"Yeah, you, too," he says. "Hey, will you come visit me tomorrow? I mean, I'm going to be so bored here, and I really liked hanging out with you."

You look at him for a second. He's pretty cute, but that tae kwon do stuff was a little goofy. Plus his parents own the camp, which could make things very awkward if it didn't work out between the two of you. You tell him ...

49

"Sure, I'll see you in the morning, first thing!" Go to 70.

"Sorry, I'm busy with my campers tomorrow." Go to 61.

"I didn't realize you were so into Joey," you explain to Missy. "If you want him that much, he's all yours as far as I'm concerned."

You both get ready for the campfire and head out the door with your campers trailing behind you. When you get there, Missy makes a beeline for Joey, and you sit with Sofie, Alice, and your other campers.

"Can I sit here?" you hear someone say. You look up to see Seth, your crush from last year!

"Of course," you say, and he sits next to you.

"Ugh, a boy!" Sofie complains, and scoots over by her best friend. As you and Seth start catching up, you notice Sofie and her friend Sky whispering about you. She's really starting to get on your nerves!

"So, are you doing this dance thing on Friday night?" Seth asks. "I mean, it's for the campers, but we can go, too," he points out.

"I don't know, I was thinking about it," you admit.

"Well, do you want to go with me?" he asks, meeting your eyes. A few hours ago, you would have said yes, instantly. But even though things didn't work out with Joey, you've now realized that there are some other guys at the camp that you might also be interested in. It's only the first day—do you want to commit to going to the dance with Seth, just because he was your crush last year, or would you rather see who else you might meet?

You say yes, you'll be his date. Go to 53.
You tell him you can't. Go to 61.

"You hardly know this guy—we both hardly know him," you point out. "And let's face it, he asked us both to the campfire. So he might like me and not you."

Missy just gives you a look and you both go back to getting dressed in silence. You pick out a short skirt, a tight white top, and your strappy sandals—the ones you were going to save for the dance on Friday.

"You're wearing THAT?" Missy asks as you look in the mirror. She's wearing jeans and sneakers. "It's a campfire, not a dance," she says. You have to admit, you *do* look a little overdressed, but maybe Missy is just jealous. You really want to get Joey's attention, and with Missy wearing jeans already, this short skirt is the only way to do it. Do you dare to wear it, or change into jeans?

You wear the sexy short skirt. Go to 56.
You dress in jeans instead. Go to 58.

$\mathcal{F}$or the rest of the week, whenever you see Seth, he's always got a big smile on his face for you. And he comes over to your table every night at dinner, just to chat for a minute.

"We're still on for Friday?" he says to you Thursday night. "For the dance?"

"Yes," you tell him. "Of course!"

When Friday comes, you spend almost an hour getting ready, and Missy and your campers help, too!

"Let me do your nails," Sofie says, getting out a bottle of red polish.

"I can do your hair," Alice offers. By the time you get to the dance, you look amazing in a summer dress and slinky sandals, with your newly painted nails. You know your campers are watching from the side of the room as Seth comes over to you. They can't wait to see what will happen—and neither can you!

"You look great," Seth says, blushing a little. "You know, I have to tell you something. I had such a bad crush on you last summer," he admits.

You're shocked. "You had a crush on *me*?" you ask him. "I had a crush on you!"

"Really?" he says. "So you won't mind if I do this…" He leans in and kisses you softly on the lips.

"Yay!" you hear Sofie yell from across the room. You look over to see your campers cheering you on. As he dances you around the room, you realize that it's going to be a pretty good summer after all—your crush is now your first kiss!

END

"Who can help us get rid of this snake?" you ask Missy.

"Seth?" Missy says, smiling. "Or Rob..."

"Please," you say, "seriously."

"Ms. Sally would know what to do," Missy admits.

She's right—Ms. Sally would be able to take care of it in no time. But this is also a good excuse to go and talk with Seth...

You decide to go to your old crush, Seth, for help. Go to 23.

You'd rather ask Ms. Sally for help. Go to 25.

$\mathcal{M}$issy is ready to go to the campfire, so she rounds up the campers. "Let's head out," she says, and the girls file into line and follow her out the door.

"I'll be there in a minute," you say, putting on some eyeliner in the mirror. Missy doesn't even act like she heard you—she's probably still mad.

You put on a little bit more makeup—just some gloss and a little blush—then fix your hair again. Finally you're ready to slip on your sandals and head out after them. You can see that you're so late, everyone else is already at the campfire. You scan the crowd for Joey, but you can't seem to find him. Then you see your camper Sofie waving at you. "We're over here!" she says, and you walk around to their side of the fire. That's when you see Joey—he's already sitting with Missy! You go right up to him and sit down on his other side. "Hi," you say, trying to act nonchalant.

"Oh, hey," Joey says, turning to look at you for a second; then he turns back to Missy. Didn't he notice how cute you look? You want to get his attention.

"It took me forever to find the right outfit for the campfire tonight," you say, looking right at Joey.

"What?" he says. "Were you talking to me?"

"I was just saying"—you straighten out your skirt and cross your legs—"I like to look nice for the campfire, you know. Jeans are so ... boring." You shoot Missy a look.

"Maybe, but why would you wear that to the campfire?" Joey says, looking at your skirt, then your top. "It looks kind of ... uncomfortable."

"Yeah," Missy says, laughing. *"Uncomfortable*, that's a good word for it."

Joey lets out a laugh and turns away from you again, back to Missy. Obviously, he's made his choice. And you feel like a ridiculous girl in an inappropriate outfit, sitting at the campfire by yourself because you no longer have a friend. Maybe you should have just worn the jeans ...

57

END

Want to change your outfit? Go to 52.

"Fine, I'll change," you tell Missy, and reach for your jeans. You throw on a T-shirt that looks good on you and slip into your sneakers.

"Ready?" Missy says curtly.

"Ready." You line the campers up to go to the campfire.

"Wait, I need some eyeliner," Sofie says.

"No, you don't," you tell her, very no-nonsense. "Let's go." You put Sofie in line with the other girls and hear her say, "Grouchy!" under her breath. You walk to the campfire with Missy and the girls in silence.

When you get there, you see Joey sitting by himself, and he waves at you. Suddenly Missy steps in front of you, almost tripping you, to get to him first. She sits right next to him, and there's no room for you.

"I was going to sit there," you say, staring her down.

"Too bad, I was here first," she says.

"Move over," you order her.

"Look," Missy says, "let's not do this." She stands up so she can whisper to you without Joey overhearing. "I don't want to fight with my best friend over some guy. Can we call a truce?"

You tell her...

ℓ

"Sorry, but I want to try for Joey, too." Go to 100.

"You're right, let's not fight over this." Go to 98.

You're about to open your mouth and tell Seth that you are scared of the ghost stories, when he says, "These stories are so dumb; nobody is scared of this stuff—I'm bored."

Now what do you do?

60

Still admit that you're a little scared. Go to 44.

Pretend that you're not scared at all. Go to 46.

$\mathcal{E}$ven though part of you regrets turning him down, you know you made the right decision.

By the time you get back to your cabin, your campers are all standing around waiting for you. Obviously, they have news.

"We just had the absolute best idea!" Christine tells you, breathlessly. "We're going to go and T.P. the boys' cabin next door!"

"I don't know what that means," Alice says shyly.

"It means that they're going to get a bunch of rolls of toilet paper and go wreck their cabin," you explain to her. "I used to do it all the time when I was a camper here. And if you want to do it right, you should also put some soap on the windows!"

"Sounds perfect!" Christine claps. "Let's go!"

"I don't think I want to," Alice says.

"She'll only do it if you help us," Christine grumbles. "She's afraid of getting into trouble. So will you? Come on, help us!"

You know the cabin they're talking about—it's the cabin where Seth is staying with his campers. Are you up for it?

Yes, you help the campers T.P. the cabin. Go to 78.

You stay out of it, but let them have their fun. Go to 81.

When you get to the lake the next morning for lifeguard training, you look around for Eric but don't see him. You're a little bummed out—why didn't he come?

"Okay everyone, let's pick a partner and get started," the instructor says. You don't know anyone else there, so you look to the girl standing next to you.

"Do you want to be partners?" she asks you.

You're about to say yes when Eric suddenly appears by your side. "Sorry, she's my partner," he says, taking your arm.

"Hey, you showed up!" you say.

"Sorry I was late—crazy campers," he explains.

The instructor starts talking about vital signs, how to check someone's breathing and pulse. "We learn this first because it's the most important thing—make sure they are breathing, that their heart is beating," he explains. He demonstrates how to check for a pulse on the wrist, and you feel your own wrist at that spot. It works! You can see that Eric is doing the same thing, his eyes on the instructor.

"Let's try the same thing on your partners now," the instructor says. Now's your chance to take Eric's hand and try to feel his pulse—it's a perfect excuse to flirt a little. Do you dare?

Yes, you take his hand. Go to 71.

No, you're too shy to be so forward with a guy. Go to 135.

The next morning, you're regretting your decision. Seth was a total jerk to you all night, and when you asked him if he wanted to do something together today, he just said, "With you? No, I'm busy," and walked off. Eric seemed like a really nice guy. Maybe you should have said yes and met Eric at lifeguard training?

You look at the clock and realize that you still have time to make it there—maybe a little bit late. You throw on your suit and race to the lake. When you get there, you can tell the instructor has already started, so you look around for Eric.

When you find him, you sit down next to him on the dock. "Hey," you say quietly.

He's surprised to see you. "I thought you weren't coming—you said you wanted to do something with Seth today," he says bitterly.

"I thought I did," you admit. "But I changed my mind."

Just then you notice a pretty blond girl sitting on the other side of Eric. She leans over. "Hi," she says. "I'm Amy."

"She's my partner for the lifeguard training," Eric says proudly.

"Oh," you say. You feel like an idiot. Of course when you turned him down, he moved on to someone else. You chose the wrong guy, and now you're left with no one.

END

Want a do-over? Go back to 44.

"Yeah, that is kind of lame," you say, laughing with Seth.

"Eric, do you need me to hold your hand?" Seth says in a baby voice. "Let me know if it gets too scary for you."

Seth turns to you to see if you're laughing at his joke. "Do you think your fat friend is scared?" he asks you, nodding over at Missy. "Maybe we should have her come over here and protect little Eric."

You look over at Missy. She did get some curves over the school year, but you would never call her fat.

"What happened to her? She really blimped out, huh?" Seth asks you, blowing his cheeks out like a puffer fish.

You want to keep joking around with Seth, but the stuff he's saying is totally mean. Do you just laugh it off, or do you tell him to stop?

He's just kidding; you laugh it off and forget it. Go to 88.

You tell him he's being kinda cruel. Go to 90.

"*A*ctually, the story is a little scary," you admit, looking at Eric. "Besides, I think it's okay to be scared sometimes."

Eric beams you a grateful look.

"Great, now I'm stuck sitting with two babies!" Seth snaps. "I'm going to get some more marshmallows. Don't pee your pants while I'm gone," he says, getting up from the log and heading to the other side of the campfire.

"Don't mind him," Eric says. "It was just a tough day with the campers today." He picks up a stick and starts poking the fire. You look over to where your campers are sitting, all huddled together talking about the ghost story, and wonder if they're going to be able to get any sleep tonight.

"That story *was* pretty scary," you say. "Maybe not the best thing right before bedtime!"

"Yeah, that part about her long wet hair covering her face … how she said, 'Who swims in my lake after dark?' Creepy!" Eric adds.

You feel a shiver go down your spine as you

look out over the lake. "You cold?" Eric asks. "Here." He takes off his jacket and puts it around your shoulders. "Let me warm up your hands," he says, trying to take your hand in his. But just then, you see Seth walking back over to your side of the fire. Even though he's been a jerk tonight, you might still have feelings for him. Do you want him to see you holding Eric's hand? Or are you totally over him?

Tell Eric you don't want to hold hands. Go to 93.

Hold hands with Eric—who cares what Seth thinks?
    Go to 124.

The next morning, you sneak out of the cabin early to head over to the infirmary. When you get there, the building is all locked up and dark—where is Gus? It's almost time to take your campers to breakfast, so you...

70

Head back to your cabin to do your job. Go to 95.
Go to his cabin to look for him. Go to 97.

You reach over and take Eric's hand. "Here, let me see if I can find your pulse," you say nervously. You look down at his wrist and try to find the place where you should put your fingers, and you can feel him watching you. Finally you place your fingers in the right place and feel his pulse. "Well, you're alive!" you say, smiling, still holding his hand in yours as you look up and meet his eyes.

"Now it's my turn," he says, taking your hand in his. He feels for your pulse and finds it quickly. "Your heart is beating fast," he whispers to you, and you feel your face turning red.

"If the pulse is too weak in the wrist, you can also use this placement in the neck," the instructor goes on, holding two fingers up to his throat. "That's the jugular. You should always be able to find a strong pulse there."

Eric lets go of your hand and reaches up to your neck, placing two fingers delicately where the instructor said to. "I have good news." He smiles. "You're alive, too."

You let out a little laugh and feel your own neck where his fingers just touched you. "Are you sitting with Seth at the campfire tonight?" he suddenly asks you.

"I don't know," you answer. "I mean, he didn't ask me to or anything."

"Do you want to sit with me?" Eric says quietly, looking you straight in the eye.

You decide to sit with Eric. Go to 83.

You're not ready to give up on Seth just yet. Go to 86.

You're pretty sure Erin was just jealous, so you decide to ignore the stuff she said about Rob. Instead, you spend the next few days getting ready for your big date. Missy and your campers help you to pick out the perfect outfit, and everyone is going to help you get ready on Friday night.

But just a couple of days before the dance, Rob suddenly seems weird around you. Maybe he's just nervous? When you see him at dinner, sometimes he seems really happy to see you, but other times it's like he doesn't even notice you're there...and then on Thursday night, you see him sitting with Erin's co-counselor, a really pretty older girl named Natalie. What if what Erin said was true? Maybe he really is a player?

"Okay, let's make you fabulous!" Sofie says, grabbing her nail polish on Friday night. She does your nails while Alice works on your makeup.

"I'm really good at eyeliner," Alice tells you quietly as she puts a black line around your eyes.

When your campers are done with you, you're

surprised to see that you actually look pretty good! "Thanks, you guys," you tell them as you slip into your summer dress. When everyone is ready, you all head out for the dance.

"You look amazing," Missy tells you, and you blush at the compliment.

When you get there, you're half-expecting Rob to be waiting for you outside, but when he's not, you're not too crushed. Maybe he wanted to meet you inside.

Your campers race in the door, excited to dance and meet some of the guys from the boys' camp. You and Missy follow them, but hang back a little to see if you can spot Rob.

"Where is he?" you whisper to her.

"Oh no," she says, pointing across the room. "There he is..." She looks at your face as you take in the scene: it's Rob all right, looking super handsome in jeans and a cool T-shirt, but he's not alone. He's standing with Natalie. Really, really close to Natalie. And whispering in her ear.

Before you can even think what to do, you watch them move to the dance floor together.

"Hey," you finally say, walking over to him. "I, uh, thought we had a date?" you ask, ready for him to explain what's going on.

"A date?" He laughs and looks at Natalie, who is giggling in a snobby way. "I'm here with Natalie," he says.

"Why don't you go and hang out with the other little girls," Natalie says, pointing across the room to where your campers are standing, watching everything.

Your legs feel numb as you walk away from him. Just then, Erin comes up alongside you. "I'm sorry, I tried to tell you he was bad news," she says, and her face looks really sad. "He did the same thing to me last summer." You feel so stupid, you can't help but burst into tears. You wish you had listened to Erin when you had the chance...

75

END

Want to take Erin's advice? Go back to 137.

After talking to Erin, you decide that maybe it's not such a great idea to go to the dance with Rob. But how can you tell him? You look across the campfire and see him sitting with his campers, roasting marshmallows and having a great time. He catches your eye and smiles big. He's so cute!

When it's time to put out the fire and go back to your cabins, you find your way over to Rob for a second. "Hey, I have to tell you something. I can't go to the dance with you on Friday," you say, looking down at your sandals. "I'm really sorry."

"Why not? Are you going with someone else?" he asks quickly.

"No, it's just that … well, you're a lot older than me. I'm just not comfortable with that," you explain. It's the truth, but you don't mention what Erin also told you.

"Okay, I understand," Rob says. He puts a finger under your chin and raises your face to look into your eyes. "How about if you let me walk you back to your cabin?" he asks.

You look around and notice that everyone else has left the campfire already, and you'll have to walk back alone. Can you trust Rob to be a good guy, or is he bad news like Erin said?

"Okay, you can walk me back." Go to 102.

"No, thanks, I can make it on my own." Go to 61.

"*O*kay," you tell the girls. "If we're going to do this, though, let's do it right! Alice: I need you to go over to the supply cabin with Sofie and Sky and get two big packs of toilet paper. And a couple bars of soap."

Alice looks happy to be included in the plan, and the girls rush out of the cabin. "The rest of you, get dressed in your darkest clothes—jeans, black tops, whatever you have." The girls get busy changing and you do the same. By the time you're all dressed, Alice, Sofie, and Sky are back, breathless. "Here," Alice says, handing you the soap. The three girls get changed quickly—except for Sofie, who always takes forever where her outfits are concerned. "I could wear my black leggings, but the only thing that looks good over those is this white skirt..." you hear her say as she's digging through her suitcase.

"Can someone give Sofie a pair of sweats or something?" you ask the other girls.

"Sweats...uh, no." Sofie pulls on a tight pair of

dark skinny jeans. "These will just have to do."
She sighs.

"You know we're just going to T.P. a cabin, right?
We're not going to a fashion show!" Alice says to
her, and you beam with pride. Alice is really getting
a backbone!

"Let's go, ladies," you say, and quietly open the
door.

You hear a couple of girls giggling. "Silence!"
you order as you all slip over to Seth's cabin.

"I'll do the windows," you whisper to the girls.
"You guys get the trees with the toilet paper." The
girls are still giggling a little bit, but you decide to
let them have their fun while you tackle the windows. You climb up on a tree stump to reach one
window and start rubbing the bar of soap all over it.
When you're almost done, a face appears in the
window—it's Seth!

"AH!" you scream, and fall backward off the
stump, right onto your butt! In a flash, he's out
the door.

"What are you guys doing?!" he yells at you.

"Calm down!" you say. "It was just a joke—"

"Well, it's not funny. And not cool. I'm telling
Ms. Sally," he snips, and runs off to the camp

director's cabin.

"What a loser!" Sofie turns to you and says. But you feel terrible. It was just meant as fun, but now Seth seems really angry with you.

You all head back to your cabin, where Ms. Sally is already waiting for you. "I cannot believe what I'm seeing," she says curtly. "I understand campers doing something like this. But counselors helping them? Soaping up windows? Honestly, girls. I don't even know what to say."

"Sorry—," you start, but Ms. Sally cuts you off.

"Save it for someone who cares! First, you will get up at five tomorrow morning and clean up the boys' cabin," she says, and your campers groan.

"QUIET!" Ms. Sally roars. "That's not all. You are not allowed to go to campfires. Or to the dance on Friday night. This whole cabin is grounded!" Ms. Sally marches off, leaving you with a group of very unhappy campers.

"Good job," Sofie grumbles as she walks by you. You've just officially ruined not only your summer but theirs, too.

END

Want to try again? Go back to 61.

"You guys go and have fun," you tell Christine and the other campers. "Just don't get caught!"

"You're not coming with us?" Alice asks you sadly.

"I can't—that kind of stuff is for campers, not counselors," you say proudly. "I'll do some laundry for the cabin instead. Who has stuff they want washed?"

Sofie quickly hands you a heap of clothes. "This much already?" you ask her.

"I wear a couple different outfits a day," she explains with a toss of her hair. You gather up the rest of the laundry from the girls and head out.

"Remember, don't get into trouble!" you warn them.

You head over to the laundry room in the dark, hoping not to run into any snakes or spiderwebs. When you get there, the room is empty and all the washers are available. You toss in the clothes and the detergent and start the machine. Then you hear the screen door creak open behind you, and you're a little startled—you spin around to see...Seth!

"Hey!" he says, obviously happy to see you. "What happened? You never showed up at the lake."

"Oh, I just..." You fumble for words. "I was so busy with the girls, I couldn't..."

"Don't sweat it," Seth says, casually. "We can hang out now, and do our laundry together."

You have to smile—he's so sweet. "I have a real fashionista in my cabin this year; she goes through clothes like crazy. I'll probably have to do laundry every night," you joke.

"In that case, I'll try to be here every night, too," Seth says, stuffing some muddy boys' clothes into the washer next to yours.

Suddenly you realize that while you two are flirting in the laundry room, his cabin is about to be covered in toilet paper and soap! Do you stall him in the laundry room and give your campers time to do a really good job, or do you confess to what's up?

Tell him about the T.P. raid. Go to 104.

Stall him and keep quiet about the raid. Go to 108.

"I'd love to sit by you," you tell Eric.

"Then I'll see you tonight," he says, smiling.

❦

That night, you take a little extra time getting ready for the campfire. You pick out a pink T-shirt that looks good on you, a little lip gloss—you find yourself really looking forward to seeing Eric. How did this happen so fast? As you head over with your campers, your head is in the clouds.

"You've got a crush!" Missy says when she sees you, poking you in the side. "Just admit it!"

You have to laugh. It's weird how quickly you got over Seth and moved on to Eric—especially since Eric isn't really your type, at least looks-wise. But he's just such a nice guy!

You get to the campfire and Eric is saving you a seat. He waves you over. "Hey, you look really nice," he says as you sit beside him. "This is for you." He shyly holds out a small wildflower. "I found it on a walk today and it made me think of you," he says, shrugging.

"I love it," you say, tucking it behind your ear. "Thanks." You look down at your sandals, then over at your campers, who are all staring at you and Eric eagerly!

"Don't look now, but we're being watched," Eric jokes.

"They aren't the only ones," you say, looking over at Seth, who is glaring at the two of you with a big scowl on his face.

"Doesn't bother me," Eric says, meeting your eyes. "I like you, and I don't care if everybody knows it—Seth, your campers, and even Ms. Sally."

You're surprised at how brave he is, and you're flattered too. It's so attractive to be confident—you feel yourself falling for him even more. As one of the older guy counselors starts telling scary ghost stories, Eric reaches for your hand, and you let him.

You sit like that for the rest of the campfire, and before you know it, it's time to go back to your cabin.

"I'll walk you," Eric says, leading you away from the campfire, still holding your hand. "So, there's this dance on Friday," he starts to say.

"I'd like to go with you," you tell him before he even has to ask.

"Good, because I'd like to go with you," he says. He stops on the trail for a second, pulling you in closer to him. It's so dark, in the moonlight you can just barely make out his face. He leans over and kisses you super softly on the lips. "So it's a date," he says quietly.

"Yes, it's definitely a date," you agree.

"Come on," he says, walking again, "your campers are going to wonder where you are." As you walk the rest of the way in silence, you realize that you have a summer boyfriend, just like that! He's not the guy you thought he would be—he's even better! Looks like it's going to be an amazing summer!

END

$\mathcal{Y}$ou like Eric, but you don't want to give up on Seth just yet. "Listen," you tell Eric, "I'd love to sit by you, but I'm kind of into someone else already..."

"Who?" he asks. "Anyone I know?"

"Actually, it's Seth," you tell him, blushing.

"Oh," he says. "I'm not saying this to hurt your feelings, but I don't think he likes you that way," Eric confesses.

"Really?" you ask, surprised. "We sort of hung out last summer," you start to tell him.

"Yeah, but he's got a girlfriend back home," Eric tells you. Then, seeing the crushed look on your face, he adds, "Oh man, I'm sorry. You didn't know?"

"Well, I wasn't that into him or anything," you start to say, but you feel your face turning red, and you're holding back tears. You can't believe Seth has a girlfriend—no wonder he was being so cold to you! And now you've blown it with Eric, too!

"Wow, awkward," Eric says under his breath. "I guess we should change partners for this training thing. You can pair up with that girl over there." He points to a girl on the edge of the group who's sitting alone. "And I guess I'll see ya," he says, unable to even meet your eyes before he walks away.

So not only is Seth taken, but you've managed to break Eric's heart, too. There goes your chance of being with a really sweet guy this summer.

END

Feel like giving it another shot? Go back to 71.

Even though Seth is being a little mean, you just laugh it off. "And what happened to her face? Are those zits or does she have poison oak?" Seth goes on. "She really got ugly over the school year!" He laughs. "Fat and ugly, not a good combination, right?" he says, turning to you.

"I don't know." You shrug. "I guess not..."

"Come on, admit it, she got fat and gross. She was cute last year," Seth points out. "Now you're the pretty one."

You don't like him talking about Missy that way—she's your friend, after all. But you don't want him to think you're lame, either. "I guess she put on a few pounds," you admit.

"A few? Try a ton!" Seth laughs, stuffing a marshmallow in his mouth. He starts to chew it up and then opens his mouth. "Hi, I'm Missy," he says in a high voice. "I like to eat!" You can't help but giggle a little bit—he's goofy and funny, even if he is making fun of your best friend.

Just then, you hear someone behind you. "Are

you making fun of me?" It's Missy, and she's heard what you guys said about her! "I was bringing you over some more marshmallows, but it looks like you've got plenty." She nods to Seth, who still has a marshmallow stuffed in his mouth.

He gulps and swallows it. "It looks like you've HAD plenty… I mean, got plenty…," he says, nudging you in the ribs. "Get it—she's *had* plenty." He laughs.

Missy looks you in the face. "I can't believe you would do this to me," she says, tears forming in her eyes. She turns and heads for the cabin, and you can hear her crying.

"You don't need that fat friend anyway," Seth says, eating another marshmallow. "Forget her." He turns back to the fire like nothing happened, and you realize that you really don't like him very much anymore, but it's a little too late now. You only hope that Missy can understand.

89

END

Want to make it up to your friend? Go back to 67.

"She's not fat," you point out. "She's just a little curvy. All the guys think she's really hot."

"Yeah, sure," Seth says. "Whatever you say. I'm going to get some more marshmallows. Don't pee your pants while I'm gone, little baby," he says to Eric, getting up from the log and heading for the other side of the fire.

"I'm sorry he was making fun of you," you tell Eric. "I should have said something."

"Don't worry about it," Eric says. "He's in a bad mood. It was just a tough day with the campers." He picks up a stick and starts poking the fire. You look over to where your campers are sitting, all huddled together talking about the ghost story, and wonder if they're going to be able to get any sleep tonight.

"That story was pretty scary," you say. "Maybe not the best thing right before bedtime!"

"Yeah, that part about her long wet hair covering her face…how she said, 'Who swims in my lake after dark?' Creepy!" Eric adds.

90

You feel a shiver go down your spine as you look out over the lake. "You cold?" Eric asks. "Here." He takes off his jacket and puts it around your shoulders. "Let me warm up your hands," he says, trying to take your hand in his. But just then, you see Seth walking back over to you. Even though he's been a jerk tonight, you still might have feelings for him. Do you want him to see you holding Eric's hand? Or are you totally over him?

Tell Eric you don't want to hold hands. Go to 93.

Hold hands with Eric—who cares what Seth thinks?
   Go to 124.

"I don't know if I'm ready for that," you admit shyly.

"No worries," Gus says. "I understand."

You two talk a little bit more as you head back to camp. When you get there, it's time for lunch with the campers. "That was fun," you tell Gus.

"Yeah," he agrees. "I'm really glad you came along."

"I guess I'll see you later," you tell him, moving to walk with your campers to the dining hall.

"You know what?" Gus says suddenly. "I was thinking maybe we could sit together at the camp-fire tonight. If you're into that. No kissing, I promise," he says, putting his hand over his heart.

"I'd love to." You smile. You're psyched that he's willing to go slow, and that he's still into you. And you're looking forward to your first date at camp!

END

"I'm okay," you tell Eric, and stand up so that you won't have to hold his hand. "I should probably get the campers back to the cabin," you explain, motioning to Missy and the girls that it's time to go.

"Okay, maybe I'll see you tomorrow?" Eric says hopefully.

"Maybe...," you tell him. You're just not sure about him yet.

On your way back to the cabin, you see the signs up on the bulletin board for tomorrow's activities. "That whitewater-rafting trip looks good," Missy points out. "'Meet Rob at the river at eight-thirty...," she reads. "Hmmmmm, our friend Rob, huh?" She winks at you.

"There's also a horseback-riding trip, with some guy named Eli leading it," you tell her, pointing at the sign.

"Oh, I know who that is," she says. "Glasses, dark hair, kinda short. I heard he's in a band or something. He's supposed to be really cool."

"Let's go already! I'm getting mosquito bites all over me!" Sofie whines.

"Well, we're trying to figure out what to do tomorrow," you tell her and the other campers. You ask the girls to take a vote—who wants to do horseback riding and who wants to go on the whitewater trip—and it's split down the middle.

"Okay, so you take three of them on one trip," Missy says, "and I'll take three on the other trip. Which one do you want?"

You look at the two signs again. Rob is really hot, but you're just not sure about the whitewater rafting. And you don't know Eli, but the horseback trip sounds fun. You decide to...

94

Go whitewater rafting to hang with Rob. Go to 32.

Try the horseback-riding trip and meet this Eli guy. Go to 141.

You're a little bummed out that you didn't get to see Gus, but it's time to take your campers to breakfast, so you head back to your cabin. On your way there, you see someone on the path—it's Gus!

"Hey, I was just going to the infirmary to meet you," he explains.

"I was just there...," you tell him.

"The nurse sent me home last night," he says. "But I didn't want to miss seeing you this morning." He blushes a little. "Anyway, what are you doing today? There's a hike later—are you taking your campers on it?"

"I don't know yet," you tell him, "I was kind of thinking about that whitewater-rafting trip today." What you don't tell him is that you're thinking about the whitewater trip because Rob, the really hot older counselor, will be running it!

"Yeah, that sounds good, but I think I'm going on the hike. If you come, we could, I don't know, walk together or something." He looks down at his sneakers shyly.

You're torn—both Gus and Rob are pretty cute, but in different ways. Who should you hang out with today?

96

Pick Rob and the whitewater trip. Go to 32.
Pick Gus and the hike. Go to 111.

You decide to head over to Gus's cabin. After all, he did say to come and visit him, didn't he? So he must want to see you.

You follow the trail, searching for the right cabin, and when you find it, the curtains are all drawn and it's dark. They're still asleep. Do you dare to knock on the door?

Let the guys sleep and see Gus later. Go to 95.
Knock on the door—you want to see him! Go to 153.

"You're right, this is dumb, no guy is worth it," you tell Missy.

She sighs, "Good. Let's just sit with our campers." She moves over to the other side of the campfire. "'Bye, Joey," she says over her shoulder.

"Yeah, 'bye," you say a little sadly. Guys come and go—you can't lose your best friend over some dude you don't even know.

After the campfire, you and Missy walk the campers back to the cabin. On your way, you see the signs up on the bulletin board for tomorrow's activities. "I heard that whitewater-rafting trip is supposed to be fun," Missy says. "It says to 'meet Rob at the river at eight-thirty,'" she reads.

"Do you think it's the same Rob?" you ask, and you feel your face turning red. You've already got such a crush on the guy!

"I *know* it's the same guy." Missy grins. "But there's also a horseback-riding trip." She points at another sign.

"With Eli," you read. "Is he that guy with the

glasses, dark hair? The one who's in a band or something? He's supposed to be really cool."

Suddenly Sofie interrupts you. "Let's go already! I'm getting mosquito bites all over me," she whines.

"Well, we're trying to figure out what to do tomorrow," you tell her and the other campers. You ask the girls to take a vote—who wants to do horseback riding and who wants to go on the whitewater trip—and it's split down the middle.

"Okay, so you take three of them on one trip," Missy says, "and I'll take three on the other trip. Which one do you want?"

You look at the two signs again. Rob is too old for you, but he's super hot. And you don't know Eli, but the horseback trip sounds fun. You decide to...

Go whitewater rafting to hang with Rob. Go to 32.
Try the horseback-riding trip and meet this Eli guy. Go to 141.

"I don't want to fight with you, either," you tell Missy. "But I think Joey is cute, and I want to sit by him."

"Even if it means that we aren't friends anymore?" Missy asks you, and she looks serious. "Because I don't want to be friends with someone who would do that to me."

"I think you're taking this a little bit too seriously—," you start to tell her.

"Don't tell me how I should feel!" Missy yells back at you, making a few heads turn at the campfire. "Ever since we got here it's been all about you—your crush on Seth, what you should wear to the campfire, and now it's about Joey, too? You're the most self-centered person I know, and I'm tired of it!" She turns and runs down the path back to the cabin.

"What's up with her?" Joey asks you.

"I don't know," you answer, but part of you wants to follow her and try to straighten out this whole thing.

"You want to sit?" Joey says, pointing to the space beside him. "They're about to start telling ghost stories."

You decide to follow Missy and straighten everything out.

Go to 155.

You sit by Joey—Missy will just have to deal with it.

Go to 157.

"Sure," you tell Rob. What harm can there be in having him walk you back to your cabin?

"Here," he says, grabbing your hand. He leads you down to the lake, away from the cabins.

"My cabin is that way," you point out to him.

"I know, I just want to take the scenic route." He smiles at you. "Spend a few minutes with you. Is that okay?"

You don't know what to say, so you just nod. He heads you down to the dock and stands with you for second, looking at the moon. You feel him turn to look at you, and he pushes your hair back from your face gently.

"You want to know a secret? I noticed you the first second I saw you in the parking lot," he tells you. "You know you're really pretty, right? I'm sure all the guys tell you that."

You're glad it's so dark out, because you can feel your face turning red. Still, you can hear Erin's words in your head—he's bad news. But he seems so sweet.

"I should get back," you tell him finally.

"Okay," he says reluctantly, and heads down the path with you, slowly, still holding your hand.

"Here's my cabin," you say, and he walks you over to the door.

"Look, if I haven't already made it clear, I'm really into you," he says as you turn to walk in. "I know you're worried about our age difference, and I can respect that. But can I just have one good-night kiss?" he asks. "Please?"

You tell him...

103

"I like you, too, but I don't want you to kiss me." Go to 61.

"Well, I guess one kiss can't hurt..." Go to 113.

"Seth, I have to tell you something, and I hope you won't be mad," you start.

He stops putting the clothes into the washer and turns to face you. "This sounds serious," he says. "What's up?"

"Well, the campers—my campers—had this idea tonight to go and T.P. a boys' cabin, and I sort of told them it would be okay," you tell him, unable to meet his eyes.

"Okay," Seth says, confused. "Why would I be mad?"

"Because the cabin they picked was..." You pause for a second. "...Yours," you say, looking up.

Seth just laughs. "You thought I'd be mad about that?" he asks. "My guys will probably love it!"

"Really?" You look into his face to be sure he's telling the truth.

"Let me just start this washer and we'll head over to make sure they don't get too out of control, though," he adds.

As you both head over to his cabin, you can see

shadows moving around quietly in the dark—it's your campers, and they are doing a killer job on the cabin. Toilet paper hangs from every branch on every tree, and the windows are all covered from top to bottom in soap.

"I'm impressed," Seth says as you near the cabin. "You've taught them well."

"It's a natural talent." You laugh.

Then, in a loud voice, he says, "Good evening, ladies!"

"AHHHHHHHH!" you hear Sofie yell.

"We're busted!" another one of your campers says, and they all scatter, dropping rolls of toilet paper and soap on the ground as they scamper to hide. Just then, a light goes on in the cabin, and a boy camper pokes his head out the door. "What...oh *man!*" he says. He's soon joined by a few other campers who also can't believe the wreckage.

"And I have some worse news for you," Seth tells his campers as they come out into the yard.

"What?" one boy asks.

"This was all done by...*girls!*"

"WHAT!?" the first boy says.

"This calls for revenge—maybe even tonight!" the other boy says.

"Not tonight. Get back into the cabin and back to bed," Seth orders. "We will discuss our revenge plans tomorrow. Right now, a spy is listening," he says, pointing over to you.

The boys glare at you as they turn and go back into the cabin, grumbling.

"A spy?" you say, laughing. "I would never..."

"I don't trust you one bit," Seth says. "Should we go put our stuff in the dryer?"

"Right," you say, but honestly you had totally forgotten about the laundry!

As you head back over to the laundry room, Seth says, "Well, since you told me a secret, and saved my cabin from being totally destroyed, I have a secret to tell you..."

"Let me guess," you say, "your campers are going to T.P. my cabin tomorrow night."

"No, well...we might, but that's not the secret. Maybe it's not even a secret, maybe you already know..." He stops walking and looks down for a second.

"What is it?" you ask, stopping on the path next to him.

He reaches over and takes your hand, still looking down.

"I had the biggest crush on you last summer," he starts, "and I still have a huge crush on you now. I guess what I'm saying is…" He stops talking and looks into your eyes.

"Oh," is all you can manage to say.

"It's okay if you don't feel the same way," Seth says, but you cut him off.

"Actually, I've had a crush on you since last summer. And I was looking forward to seeing you here this summer. I know that sounds dumb—"

Before you can finish, he leans in and kisses you softly on the lips.

"Nothing about you is dumb," he says quietly. "I don't date dumb girls."

You smile. "Does this mean we're dating?"

"It does, if you want to be," he says.

And you do.

END

"Well," you say, "I guess I should go check on my campers."

"If you want to wait until I'm done loading this wash, I'll walk back with you," Seth offers.

You would love to walk with him, but not tonight! When you round the bend in the path, he's going to see all your campers destroying his cabin—and he's not going to be very happy!

"No, that's okay," you say, scrambling for an excuse. "I've got to, uh, I'm in a hurry. I'll see you later." You back out the screen door and run down the path to your cabin. When you get there, the cabin is empty—the girls must still be T.P.'ing the boys' cabin. You sit on your bunk for a second, then hear something outside. The door swings open and your campers tumble back in.

"We did it!" Sofie yells. "You should have seen it!"

"We really wrecked their cabin," Alice offers. It's the first time you've seen her look happy since she got here. As the girls start telling you everything they did, there's a knock on the door.

You all fall silent.

"Uh-oh," Sofie says. "Busted!"

"Pretend to be asleep!" you whisper to them. The girls scramble for their beds and you open the door.

It's Seth. "Hey, you forgot your bottle of detergent in the laundry room," he tells you, handing it to you.

"Oh, that's so nice of you!" you say, surprised that he isn't there to complain about the T.P. raid. "Uh, let me come outside, the girls are sleeping," you lie, pulling the door closed behind you.

"Are they really?" Seth says, smiling. "That's funny, because I could have sworn I just saw them over at my cabin, rubbing soap on the windows and throwing roll after roll of toilet paper into the trees. But maybe I'm wrong..."

You look down, embarrassed. "Look, I'm sorry, I almost told you, I just..."

"Don't worry about it," Seth says, meeting your eyes. "Really, it's just camp stuff, right?"

"You're not mad?" you ask him.

"Do I look mad?" he says, locking eyes with you. You missed an opportunity to tell him a secret earlier in the night, and now is your big chance to

109

make up for it—by telling him that you like him. The moment is right, so do you confess, or keep it inside?

Tell him you like him. Go to 115.
Keep quiet about it. Go to 117.

$\mathcal{C}$ecile, the older girl counselor who is leading the hiking trip, gives very strict instructions at the trailhead. "Stick together, counselors; please keep an eye on your campers. And most important: no going off the path. There's poison ivy, poison oak, and snakes out there, okay?" Everyone is paying attention—snakes? No, thanks!

"You don't have to worry about that," Gus whispers to you. "I'll protect you," he says, jumping into one of his tae kwon do positions. "Aḣ-YAY!" he shouts. A few of the campers shoot him a weird look.

"Do you really think that would scare a snake?" you ask him, laughing.

"I am a master of the martial arts," Gus jokes. "Snakes can smell it on me and will stay away in fear!"

You laugh—Gus is definitely kinda silly, but you love hanging out with him.

The hike is really beautiful, through a part of the forest you've never been in. And Cecile keeps pointing out cool stuff, like really old trees that were here before our grandparents were born, and weird plants called fiddleheads. "These plants actually roll up into a ball at night, and then open again when the sun comes out," Cecile explains. "And see this bug?" she says, pointing to a gross-looking brown beetle. "You can eat these. They're full of protein! Might want to keep that in mind if you're ever lost in the woods."

"E*wwwww*," you say, turning to Gus, and he makes a face back at you.

At one point, Gus pulls you to the side, away from the group. "Hey, you wanna go see this secret waterfall I know about?" he asks. "It's just over here."

"We're not supposed to go off the trail," you say.

He gives you a look. "Come on, she just said that for the kids. We're counselors—we can do what we want," he says.

"I don't want to get in trouble," you say, watching as the group moves down the trail, away from you.

"You won't," Gus says. "Anyway, my parents own the camp. How much trouble could we get in?"

You decide to go off the path with him and see the waterfall.
    Go to 118.

You skip the waterfall and stay on the hike. Go to 143.

"*O*kay," you say quietly, looking down.

He puts his hands on your face and moves in to kiss you. This first kiss is soft, on your lips, then another, and another. But suddenly his hands move down to your back, and he's kissing you pretty hard on the mouth—in a way that you haven't really done before, and he's pushing your back against the door. Just then, the door opens behind you and you both tumble into the cabin!

"Ow!" you say, landing right on your butt, hard. Rob almost falls right on top of you.

"What the—," he says, looking up.

You both see who opened the door from inside—it's Ms. Sally—and she doesn't look happy!

"Your campers were worried about you," she tells you sternly. "I can see now that they didn't need to be. You were in very good hands with Robert here, weren't you?" She glares at you both.

"We were just...," you start to say.

"Oh, I know exactly what you were doing. You were out past curfew. You weren't with your campers when you were supposed to be. And you were enjoying the male advances of another counselor, in clear view of these impressionable young ladies," Ms. Sally says. You hear Sofie snicker at the mention of being "impressionable."

"What kind of an example do you think you're setting for them?" Ms. Sally asks you.

"I...I don't know," you say, at a loss for words.

"The right thing to do in this situation is to dismiss you from your duties at this camp," she announces. "Robert, return to your cabin and pack your things. And you do the same." She points at you. "I'll call your parents to come and pick you up."

Rob sulks out of the cabin, leaving you to pack under the watchful eye of Ms. Sally. Looks like your first camp kiss will be your last!

114

END

Want to stay at camp a little longer? Go back to 102.

"There's something else I should probably tell you, while I have the chance," you say, feeling your heart start to beat fast. "I, um..."

"You're going to T.P. my cabin again tomorrow night?" Seth guesses, laughing.

"No, it's just that I...well, I had a crush on you all last summer," you finally say, the words coming out in a rush. "And I think I might have another crush on you this summer."

It takes you a few seconds even to look up, and when you do, Seth is just standing there, looking at you like you're crazy or something.

"Okay, well, I guess I'm going to go to bed," you finally say, feeling stupid. Maybe confessing was a huge mistake.

"Wait," Seth says, grabbing your hand. "I can't believe that...because I had a huge crush on *you* all last summer," he admits. "I actually called Ms. Sally this year to see if you were going to be back as a junior counselor before I signed up to do the job!"

"You did?" you ask him, smiling.

"Yeah," he says quietly. "So what do we do now?" he asks.

"I don't know," you admit shyly. "I guess next time my campers are going to wreck your cabin, I could warn you." You laugh.

"That would be nice," Seth says, smiling. "And I guess we could go to the dance on Friday and see what happens."

"That would also be nice," you tell him, looking into his eyes.

"It's a date, then," he says, squeezing your hand.

You can hardly believe that your huge summer crush is actually your date! Looks like your summer is off to a pretty amazing start!

END

"Guess I'll see you later," Seth says, lingering around for a minute or two. You almost tell him your secret, but then you can't, just like last year.

"Okay, 'bye," you finally say, going into your cabin. By now the girls are all almost asleep, so you go to sit on your bunk and get out your journal. As you write about the day, you start feeling really bad about the missed opportunity to tell Seth how you feel. Why is it so hard for you to talk to boys sometimes? It's something that you really need to work on. You write out a whole pretend dialogue that you wish you had been able to have with Seth, then turn out the light and lie in your bunk. Is it going to be another summer just like last year? Always crushing on a guy from a distance but never actually having a boyfriend…?

END

Want to try again? Go back to 108.

117

"This way," Gus says, grabbing your hand and leading you into the woods. Pretty soon, you're so far off the trail you're not sure you'll know how to get back.

"Do you know where we're going?" you ask him.

"Yeah, it's right over…" Gus looks to his left. "Or maybe it's this way," he says, pulling you after him. A sharp, thorny bush catches your arm. "Ow!" you yell, looking down to see blood on your hand and arm.

"You're okay," Gus grumbles. "Come on." He's being kind of a jerk, pulling you through the bushes and thorns.

"Hmmmmm," Gus says, stopping for a second. "I could've sworn it was right over here. Let's try this way," he says, turning left again.

You've been walking for a long time, and you're starting to get thirsty and hungry. "I think we should turn back," you finally say to Gus after another hour of walking around in circles.

"They're going to be worried about us, don't you think?"

"I guess so," Gus says. "We just have to figure out which way is back to the trail."

"Are we lost?" you ask him.

"No, no, I'm sure I can find it," he tells you. You're starting to realize that Gus is a lot of talk and jokes but not really someone who can be counted on.

"Great," you say sarcastically. Your legs and arms are all scratched up from thorns and branches, and as the sun starts to go down, you realize that you haven't eaten since breakfast. And you're not about to eat bugs!

Finally, when you're just too tired to go on any-more, you sit down for a second, under a tree. It's getting dark by this point, and you're a little worried that you're going to have to spend the night out in the woods. Just then, you hear someone calling your name—and Gus's. It's a search party! They've found you!

"Boy, are you guys in a lot of trouble," says the older guy counselor, shining his flashlight in your face. "Ms. Sally is not happy. Follow us back to camp," he orders, leading the way. So much for the waterfall adventure—and your perfect summer.

END

Want to see what happens if you stay on the path?
   Go back to 111.

You climb up into the saddle, and before you can even get your feet in the stirrups, Irish starts prancing around, gunning to go. She moves fast for the barn door, and you don't know what to do! You feel like you're about to fall off—"HELP!" you yell, and hear Sofie snicker as your horse races from the stables. Suddenly, Eli moves up alongside you on his horse and pulls the reins from your hands. "Whoa, Irish!" he orders, and the temperamental horse stops.

"Are you sure you want to take this horse? She really can be difficult," Eli explains, looking you in the eye. "We're going on a long ride, so you might want to reconsider."

You decide to stay on the hard horse. Go to 148.
You'd rather switch to the easier horse. Go to 147.

"I guess so...," you answer hesitantly.

"Cool," he says. Then he leans over and quickly kisses you on the cheek.

"Hey, I thought you said not now!" You laugh, surprised.

"Yeah, I changed my mind," he says with a grin. Just then you notice that Sofie is looking back, watching you guys.

"Uh, gross!" she says, then starts whispering to her best friend.

"We're being watched," Gus whispers in your ear.

"I noticed that," you say back, but honestly you don't really care. You're into this guy, so what's to be embarrassed about?

"I wonder what they're going to say when they see us sitting together at the campfire tonight," Gus says to you.

"Are we sitting at the campfire together tonight?" you ask him.

"Oh, are you asking me on a date?" he jokes. "My answer is yes. I'll see you there." He smiles.

"Very sneaky!" You giggle. You have to admit, there's something special about Gus—he's smart and funny and he totally cracks you up. When you get back to camp, he takes your hand in his and kisses it. "I'll see you tonight," he says as he walks away. Who knew that a little poison oak would lead to romance?

END

You slip your hand into Eric's even though you see Seth coming back over to sit down. He looks at you but doesn't say anything.

When you look over at Eric, you notice something—maybe it's just the light from the fire, but he's suddenly looking so much cuter to you. Why has it taken you so long to notice this guy?

"What are you doing tomorrow?" he asks you, giving your hand a squeeze. "Are you going to try the lifeguard training? Or are you doing something else?"

Honestly, you had been hoping to do whatever Seth was doing, get to hang out with him a little bit. But now you're not so sure. Are you ready to give up on Seth and do something with Eric, or do you give Seth a second chance?

Say yes to lifeguard training. Go to 63.
Tell Eric you sort of have plans with Seth. Go to 65.

$\mathcal{B}$y the time you get your campers over to the cabin, you're already regretting your decision.

One little girl comes over to you crying, "That girl took the bunk I wanted!"

"Okay...," you say, looking at her name tag, "Alice. Let's find you another bunk."

"No, I wanted that one, and she took it!" Alice wails.

"You're a baby. Why don't you go stay in the baby cabin," a girl with long red nails yells at her.

"Sofie, you're mean," another girl chimes in.

"Nobody talk to Sofie until she says she's sorry," a little girl named Christine says.

"Shut up, Christine, what do you know?" Sofie fires back.

"GIRLS!" you finally yell. "Let's not fight! We just got here. How can we work this out—maybe flip a coin or something?"

"Oh please," Sofie says, rolling her eyes. "Nobody talk to the counselor, because she's a loser." You hear a few of the campers laugh and realize that you are totally losing control of the situation. You could run next door, to Seth's cabin, and ask for help, or try to get your campers to behave on your own. You decide to...

Go next door for help. Go to 130.

Try to take care of the crisis yourself. Go to 127.

"I want each of you to write down your name on a piece of paper," you order. "Then I'm going to put your names into a hat. The first name I draw out gets to pick her bunk, and so on until everyone has a bed, and that's how we're going to pick bunks." You're pretty proud of yourself for thinking up a solution to the crisis.

"I think that's dumb," Sofie grumbles.

"No one cares what you think," Christine snips, pushing her long blond hair back. "She's the counselor; we have to do what she says."

"You just want my bunk because I got here first and got the best one," Sofie yells at Alice. "I'll do the names in a hat thing," Sofie says, turning to you. "But Alice *cannot* have this bunk—that's the only rule." Sofie sits down on a bed and crosses her arms. She looks really pissed.

"That's totally not fair!" Alice yells, looking at you. "Tell her she can't have that bunk! It's not fair!"

"Yeah!" Christine yells, and pretty soon, they're

all fighting again. Just then, you notice someone standing in the doorway—it's your crush from last year, Seth!

"Is everything okay over here? I heard some yelling and thought I'd better come over," he says.

The girls don't even notice him and just keep on fighting with each other.

"Oh, we're fine, just trying to pick bunks." You sigh. "How are you? How was your school year?" You're so psyched to see him, but you wish he had shown up at a better time!

"It was okay," he says. "Are you sure you want to let them do that?" he says, pointing at Christine, Sofie, and Alice, who are now practically wrestling, pushing and shoving each other.

"Girls, come on!" you yell, separating them.

"Maybe you should have waited another year to become a junior counselor," Seth says snidely, hurting your feelings. "Do you think you've got this under control?" he asks, turning to leave.

"Yeah, I can handle it," you lie. You want to tell him to mind his own business—what makes him think he's so qualified to be a junior counselor and you're not?

"So maybe I'll see you at the campfire later?" he

asks. "I mean, if you can keep your campers from killing each other."

The way he's acting, you're not so sure you want to hang out with him later. You have to think fast, before the girls tear each other apart, so you say...

129

"Sure, I'll see you there." Go to 27.

"I'll have to see if I can make it." Go to 29.

"Hold tight for just a minute," you tell your campers, and run out the door to the nearest cabin—the boys' cabin. You're hoping to knock on the door and see Seth, but when you get there, you see Rob—the guy who helped you load the bus earlier—standing outside.

"Hey, there," he says, looking at you. "Everything okay?" He meets your eyes for a second, and you feel totally tongue-tied—in fact, you almost forget why you came over in the first place.

"Oh…no, everything isn't okay. My campers are acting crazy, fighting over bunks, I don't know…" You realize you're talking really fast, and stop for a second.

"Don't worry about it," Rob says. "I just came over here to help Seth and Eric get their campers settled. It happens." He comes over to you and puts his arm around your shoulders. "Let's head back to your cabin and show them who's boss, okay?" You love how his arm feels around you, and find yourself smiling up at him. When you get back to the cabin, Sofie is still planted on the bunk she's claimed, and Alice is trying to pull her off.

"Ladies," Rob says, and everyone turns, surprised to see a guy in their cabin.

"Hello," Sofie says, flipping her long hair. For a nine-year-old, she really knows how to flirt!

"Both of you want that bunk, huh?" Rob says. "Here's what we're going to do: I'm thinking of a number between one and a hundred. You two are each going to guess a number, and whoever is closest gets to have the bunk…for the first week of camp. Then you trade. Got it?"

Both girls nod, obviously taken with Rob. As it turns out, Alice guesses the closest, but Sofie is fine with it—that, or there's no way she's going to act immature in front of Rob. As he turns to leave, you whisper to him, "I don't know how to thank you!"

He just smiles at you. "Come to the campfire with me tonight," he says.

"Uh," your mind is spinning—Rob is a few years too old for you to be dating him, but he is so hot, maybe it would be okay…You tell him,

"Okay, I'd love to! See you there." Go to 150.

"No, but thanks, though." Go to 29.

You just can't take the humiliation anymore! You climb down off of Daisy and, without saying anything to Eli or your campers, race back to your cabin, where you can cry in peace. You get out your journal and write down everything that happened to you—where did you go wrong? Why is your summer so awful? Why is everyone picking on you? You sit and cry until it's almost time for the campers to come back from their trip, debating whether or not you should just go to Ms. Sally and quit. How can you face Sofie and the other campers again? So far, your summer is horrible!

132

END

Want to start all over again? Go to 10.

ou decide you're not in the mood to fight with a college girl over some guy you just met—no matter how hot he is! So you move to the other side of the campfire, where your campers are sitting, and sit by Missy and another junior counselor named Eli—a sorta cute guy with big funky glasses and super short dark hair.

"I'm doing this horseback-riding trip tomorrow," he tells you and Missy. "You guys should come— we're going to ride for a while, then do a picnic. It should be really cool."

Just then, Rob appears next to you. "Hey, I thought we were going to sit together," he says, shooting a look at Eli.

"Me, too," you tell him. "But I guess Natalie got there first."

"Oh, her...," Rob says. "Yeah, whatever. Look, what are you doing tomorrow? I'm running this whitewater-rafting trip that is going to be amazing. Come with me—bring your campers," he says, meeting your eyes. "I promise you'll have fun."

Rob is amazingly hot, and you love that he's paying attention to you right now, but he's older and it really bothered you that he didn't stand up for you when Natalie sat next to him. But maybe you should give him a second chance? Or there's always the horseback-riding picnic with Eli, who seems really nice…

You choose the whitewater trip with Rob. Go to 32.

You decide to do the horseback-riding trip with Eli.

Go to 141.

You're way too shy to reach over and just grab his hand, so instead you listen to the instructor and keep your eyes forward.

"Okay, now let's practice this with our partners—take your partner's wrist and see if you can find the pulse point," the instructor says. "Let's see who can do it quickly—remember, in an emergency, time is all you have."

"You want to go first?" Eric says, holding out his wrist to you.

"No, that's okay," you say. You're afraid even to look at him.

He reaches for your hand. "Then I'll try on you," he says quietly. When his hand touches yours, you feel yourself pulling back.

"What, do I have a disease or something?" Eric jokes. "I have to touch you to get your pulse."

"We've got it!" the team next to you says. They're already done, and you haven't even started.

"Guess it doesn't matter now," you mumble, hiding your hands in your lap.

"Is something wrong?" Eric says. "Do you want to be partners with someone else?"

"No, it's not that," you start to explain. "I guess I just get shy sometimes." You look down, blushing.

"That's okay," Eric says, sounding relieved. "I like that about you. I think we need to hang out more; then you won't be so nervous."

You just nod, unable to meet his eyes.

"How about if we meet at the campfire tonight and sit together?" he asks.

You're ready to get to know Eric better, so you say yes.
Go to 83.

You're not quite ready to give up on Seth or to move things forward with Eric. Go to 86.

That night at the campfire, you're still thinking about your upcoming date with Rob when an older counselor comes over to you.

"Can I talk to you for a second?" she asks you, and you recognize her from the first day at camp— her name is Erin.

"Sure," you say, and she takes a seat next to you.

"I heard that you're going to the dance on Friday with Rob," she says, pushing back her long black hair. "True?"

"Um, I guess so," you admit.

"I wanted to warn you, he's bad news," she says. "You better watch yourself." You can tell from the look on her face that she's dead serious.

"What do you mean?" you ask her. Rob seems great—even if he is a lot older than you.

"Just trust me, you're too young to be going out with him. So don't," she says, then gets up and moves back over to sit with her friends. You...

Still go to the dance with him on Friday. Go to 73.

Take her advice and tell him you can't be his date. Go to 76.

You're about to open your mouth and tell Seth that you're not scared at all, when he says, "Because if you are scared, I could walk you back to your cabin tonight."

138

Pretend that you are scared in order to get attention from him. Go to 44.

Tell him the truth, that you're not scared at all. Go to 46.

"Who do you think you ARE?" you say loudly, getting in Natalie's face.

"I'm not about to get into a fight with a little girl like you," Natalie says, giving you a shove.

"Don't touch me!" you yell at her, shoving her back—hard. She loses her balance and falls backward off the log where she was sitting by Rob.

"Are you crazy?" Natalie asks you, standing up and brushing off her shorts. She turns to Rob and says, "Did you see that? She just hit me!"

"I didn't hit you," you snarl at her. "But I'm about to!"

"Ladies, ladies," Rob says. "Don't fight. There's plenty of me to go around!" He gives you a wink and then looks at Natalie with a sly smile. Suddenly you realize that he set you both up to think that you were going to be his "date" at the campfire tonight—what a jerk! He's a total dog!

You turn and storm off to get some air, feeling like a total loser—now you've got no guy and you embarrassed yourself in front of everyone at the campfire. How will you ever show your face at Camp Butterfield again? There goes *any* chance of having a boyfriend this summer.

END

Want to try again? Go back to 150.

When you get to the barn for the horseback ride the next morning, all the horses are already saddled up—Eli is one organized guy!

"Look at this!" Sofie points out, "He's got saddlebags on each horse packed with picnic stuff, too."

"This is going to be so fun!" another camper says.

You're happy you picked this activity today, especially when Eli comes around the corner. He's looking really cute in jeans and a white T-shirt—and cowboy boots?

Whatever, it looks good on him, even with his funky glasses and rocker dude haircut.

"I'm letting everyone pick their own horses," he explains to the group, and all of the boy and girl campers scatter, everyone grabbing the reins of the horse they want.

You spot a pretty white horse that no one has claimed. "I'll take this one. What's his name?"

"It's a she," says Eli. "Her name is Irish, and she's tough—better for a more experienced rider."

"I've got five years of riding," Sofie says snottily. "I can take her; you can have this horse instead." She points to an old-looking, drab gray horse.

"Yeah, Daisy is probably a better horse for you," Eli says. But you're not so sure. Are you going to be shown up by your spoiled little camper? Everyone is watching to see what you will do, so you ...

Take the easy horse, Daisy. Go to 145.
Take the harder horse, Irish. Go to 121.

"I'd love to see the waterfall, but I have to stay with my campers right now," you tell Gus. "You know, I'm in charge of them and everything."

"That's cool," Gus says. "Maybe another time, when we're hiking without our campers."

When it's time to turn around and head back to camp, Gus stays with you, walking behind your group of campers. "So, I have a question for you," he says at one point when the campers are out of earshot. "Do you have a boyfriend?"

You have to laugh. "No," you tell him quickly.

"Good, because I would hate to have to fight him for you," he jokes, putting up his hands in a martial-arts position. "These hands are lethal weapons, you know," he adds.

"So I've heard." You laugh.

"And now I have another question," Gus says, walking close beside you. "Since you don't have a boyfriend, would it be okay if I kissed you sometime—maybe not now, but sometime?"

Gus is funny and cool, but are you into him that way? You tell him . . .

"Yes, you can kiss me." Go to 122.

"No, I don't think so." Go to 92.

ou climb up into Daisy's saddle and find out you have a problem. "Let's go, giddy up!" you tell her, urging her sides with your feet. But the horse acts like you're not even there—she's ignoring you and standing totally still, while everyone else is on their way down the trail.

"Hold up, everyone," Eli yells, noticing that you aren't with the group. "What's wrong?" he yells back to you.

"I don't know; she won't move!" you tell him.

You hear Sofie laughing and saying something to the other campers about you—then you hear them all laughing, even the boys in the group. For a nine-year-old, she really knows how to be annoying!

Eli circles back and gives Daisy an encouraging nudge. "Come on, girl," he coaxes her. You like how he's so great with the horses. Finally, Daisy takes a few steps, then stops again. And then the smell hits you …

"Oh, that's the problem!" Eli says. "She had to

go," he explains as you hear a big, wet *plop*. Your horse is pooping on the trail!

"Gross!" you hear Sofie yell. "That smells so bad! Your horse is disgusting!"

You've just about had it with this whole horseback-riding thing—and with Sofie—and you're ready to call it quits. How can you go on a riding trip now?

You decide to jump off Daisy and go back to your cabin—forget this! Go to 132.

You take a deep breath (plugging your nose, of course!), and stay cool. Go to 151.

"You know what, I think I'd better switch to the easier horse," you have to admit.

"This horse will be much better for you," Sofie says with her know-it-all tone. "It takes an experienced rider to understand how to handle a difficult horse." You can tell the other campers are looking at her with respect and it really bothers you. That's how they're supposed to look at you!

147

Go to 145.

"I think I can handle it," you tell Eli, and stay on Irish.

"Okay, if you say so," Eli says. "Let's go campers!" he yells, rounding up everyone and their horses and heading down the trail.

Even though riding Irish is a nightmare, there's no way you're going to let Sofie—a little nine-year-old brat—show you up in front of your campers and Eli. Forget it!

Sofie clearly knows what she's doing and moves her horse into lead position on the trail, ahead of everyone else. You hate to admit it, but she looks good on horseback—very confident and tall.

Irish keeps pulling to the side and won't obey anything. Sometimes it seems like she wants to race ahead of the other horses, but other times she stops to munch a little bit of grass on the edge of the trail and you can barely get her moving. You can't wait until you can stop for lunch and get off this crazy horse.

At one point, after you've been on the trail

about an hour, Irish stops around the bend for a munch of grass and wildflowers and she just won't get going again, so Eli has to stop and circle back for you. "You okay?" he calls back. "Just give her a good kick and she'll listen to you," he says. At this point you're so tired of dealing with this horse that you decide you will give her a good kick. You pull your feet back hard into her ribs—and the next thing you know you're flying through the air! You land on your butt with a hard *thump* and instantly hear the laugher of the campers around you.

"Maybe not that hard." Eli laughs. Your butt is killing you as you stand up. "Ow," you complain, rubbing your seat.

"I knew she couldn't handle that horse," Sofie says, turning her horse and heading back onto the trail.

"Our counselor is so lame!" you hear another girl say.

END

Maybe you should have gone on the easy horse after all.

Go to 121.

149

When you get to the campfire that night, you notice a really pretty older counselor talking to Rob. Actually, you remember her from earlier: it's Erin's friend Natalie. You get your campers seated and move over to sit by Rob, but just as you're about to sit, Natalie scoots over, leaving you no room.

"I was going to sit there," you tell her, even though you're pretty sure she already knew that and did it on purpose.

"Too bad," she says, and turns back to Rob, ignoring you.

"Look, Natalie, or whatever your name is," you say loudly, "Rob asked me to sit by him at campfire tonight, so that's my seat. Move."

You're feeling pretty good about yourself for standing up to her.

"No," she says simply, and turns back to Rob, who is just ignoring you both.

You decide to confront her and sit by Rob. Go to 139.

You'd rather just sit somewhere else. Go to 133.

"I can't deal with this!" you tell Eli and laugh. "Can I just ride with you or something?"

"Great idea," he says, giving you his hand. "We'll tie Daisy's reins up here and she'll just follow along with us."

You jump up on the back of his horse and wrap your arms around him, shooting Sofie a smug look. Now Eli can do all the work, and you can enjoy the ride without embarrassing yourself too much in front of your campers. And you get to hang with Eli, which isn't too bad, either!

After about an hour on the trail, Eli has everyone stop and tie up their horses near a big field of wildflowers, where you'll all have lunch. You and Eli sit together, but you notice Sofie giving you the evil eye. Maybe that's the problem—it's not that she doesn't like you; she's got a little crush on Eli!

"So are you going to the movie tonight?" Eli asks.

One night a week, they show a movie outside

for the whole camp. You were hoping to find Seth there tonight, your crush from last year, and maybe sit with him. But if Eli wants to sit together...

You say yes. Go to 159.

You tell him you're hoping to sit with Seth. Go to 161.

You raise your hand to knock on the door, then hesitate. Is he going to be mad if you wake him up? Who cares—he's the one who told you to come and visit him, and he *did* say "in the morning," right?

You knock on the door but hear nothing from inside. After a minute, you knock again, harder this time, and hear some voices from inside. A bleary-eyed guy comes to the door. "Yeah, what?" he says, looking at you. He's clearly still half-asleep.

"Is Gus here?" you ask him.

"Uh, I guess," the guy says, turning around and heading back into the cabin. You hear him say, "Gus, some girl is at the door for you."

In a minute, Gus is at the door. His hair is standing up all over the place and he's in pajamas.

"Uh, what...who...what are you doing here?" he asks you, and you can hear someone laughing from inside the cabin.

"You said to come and visit you, and I went to the infirmary," you start to explain.

"The nurse sent me home last night," he says,

looking at you strangely. "What's your name again?" he asks you, and you hear more laughter from inside.

"Forget it," you say, totally embarrassed. You run back to your cabin, mortified. How could you have been such an idiot—he didn't even remember your name! You wish you could just go back and start this whole day over again—and not be such a dork next time!

END

Want to rethink that move? Go back to 97.

You race down the path and catch Missy on her way into the cabin. She's crying pretty hard. "Missy! Wait!" you yell after her.

"Just leave me alone!" she yells back.

You catch up to her. "Look, I just wanted to say I'm sorry. Maybe I have been a little selfish. I just didn't realize that you were that into Joey."

Missy looks up at you with tears in her eyes.

"If you like him that much, of course I'm not going to make a move on him," you explain. "Our friendship is way too important to me."

"Okay," Missy says, sniffling. "I'm sorry, too. I didn't mean to yell at you in front of everyone."

"Let's forget about it and head back to the campfire, what do you say?" You look at her blotchy face.

She just nods with a sniffle. You two head back to the campfire, talking a little bit more. On your way, you see the signs up on the bulletin board for tomorrow's activities.

"That whitewater-rafting trip looks good," Missy

points out. "'Meet Rob at the river at eight-thirty,'" she reads. "Hmmmmm, our friend Rob, huh?" She winks at you.

"There's also a horseback-riding trip with some guy named Eli leading it," you tell her, pointing at the sign.

"Oh, I know who he is," she says. "Glasses, dark hair, kinda short. I heard he's in a band or something. He's supposed to be really cool."

"Since we have six campers, I guess you could take three of them on one trip," Missy says, "and I'll take three on the other trip. Which one do you want?"

You look at the two signs again. Rob is too old for you, but he is super hot. And you don't know Eli, but the horseback trip sounds fun. You decide to...

Go whitewater rafting to hang with Rob. Go to 32.

Try the horseback-riding trip and meet this Eli guy.

Go to 141.

You sit down next to Joey, feeling a little guilty. Just then, an older guy counselor gets up and starts telling a ghost story—it's about a creature that lives in the woods on the border of the camp. And it only comes out when it sees a campfire burning bright. You feel a shiver go down your spine and you snuggle a little closer to Joey. You wish he would hold your hand or something.

"This is scary, huh?" you finally ask him.

"Yeah," he says back, not taking his eyes off the counselor. You decide to reach over and try to hold his hand, since he's not going to make a move. After all, you just ruined your friendship with Missy over this guy, so something better happen!

As you grab his hand, he pulls back. "Oh, sorry, I, uh, I can't do that," he says, looking sheepish.

"Why not?" you ask him.

"I've got a girlfriend," he says quickly. "She wouldn't like it. Besides, I just don't like you that way, okay?"

Ugh. Too bad you can't do this whole night over again.

END

158

Want to rewind? Go to 58.

That night, you go to the movie with your campers, but you're looking for Eli. It's pretty dark, and you're afraid you won't find him, so you finally just sit with your campers up front.

"I'm so excited for movie night," Alice, your shy camper, tells you. "Aren't you?"

You want to tell her yes, but honestly, you can't stop thinking about Eli. Is he going to show up or not?

Just then, you see him—and he sees you! He's still wearing the jeans and cowboy boots from earlier, but with a different shirt. You feel a huge grin spread across your face as he heads over to your group. "Okay if my campers sit here, too?" he asks you.

"Of course!" you tell him, and he calls his group over.

"Yuck—boys!" you hear Alice say, rolling her eyes. You decide just to ignore her.

"Here," Eli says, spreading out a big blanket. "I brought this for us...I mean for everybody."

You look at him, and he shyly looks away. He's a great guy, and you're so glad you decided to sit by him. During the movie, he reaches over and takes your hand quietly, without saying anything, and looks into your eyes for a second. You give him a smile, then look back to the movie. You realize you've already had your perfect movie ending!

END

You like Eli, but you're not quite ready to give up on Seth just yet. "Listen," you tell Eli, "I'd love to sit by you, but I'm kind of into someone else already."

"Who?" he asks. "Anyone I know?"

"Actually, it's Seth," you tell him, blushing.

"Oh, I know Seth," he says. "I'm not saying this to hurt your feelings, but I don't think he likes you that way," Eli confesses.

"Really?" you ask, surprised. "We sort of hung out last summer," you start to tell him.

"Yeah, but he's got a girlfriend back home," Eli tells you. "And he's really into her."

You look down, totally embarrassed. "Oh, well, I mean, I wasn't that into him or anything..." You feel your face turning red. What an idiot! No wonder Seth was acting so cold to you. And now you've blown it with Eli, too!

"But I know what it's like to have a crush on someone," Eli says. "That's cool. Don't worry about it." He gets up to clean up after the campers and get everyone back on their horses. You watch him moving around the group, chatting with everyone, being super sweet, and you're already regretting your choice. There goes your chance of being with a really great guy this summer.

END

Want to make a different choice? Go back to 151.

CYLIN BUSBY

first chose a life as a book and magazine editor, before going back a page and becoming a full-time writer instead. She lives with two boys of her own choosing—Damon, her husband, and August, her son, in Los Angeles.

ready for a few new boys to choose from?

Check out:

Date Him or Dump Him?
The Dance Dilemma

The junior homecoming dance is right around the corner. Do you join the decorating committee to meet some potential dates, or hit the mall in search of the perfect dress? And at every turn, there is the question of your date. Will you land the guy you want? Or will you go to the dance alone—if you go at all?

Available August 2007

And don't miss:

Date Him or Dump Him?
Ski Trip Trouble

Will you ski the slopes or cuddle up close? The choice is yours!

Coming in Fall 2007